CONFLICT OF INTEREST

THE WALKER FIVE, BOOK 1

MARIE JOHNSTON

Conflict of Interest

Copyright 2017 by Marie Johnston

Developmental Editing by Razor Sharp Editing

Copyediting by The Killion Group

Proofing by HME Editing

Cover design by Shannon of Shanoff Designs

The characters, places, and events in this story are fictional. Any similarities to real people, places, or events are coincidental and unintentional.

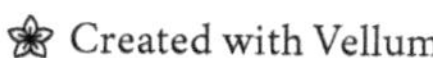 Created with Vellum

After returning home from the Army, Dillon honors his father's last request to get help for his "drinking problem," but it's a waste of time. He has other matters to worry about than the few beers he has after work…every day.

When Dillon Walker swaggers into Elle Brady's office, she fully understands the appeal of a small-town farm boy. He's handsome, charming, helps run his family's successful farm and ranch, and he's definitely interested in her. Too bad she's an addiction counselor still caring for her recovering alcoholic father, and she's more than gun-shy of someone with Dillon's baggage.

Elle scraps their professional relationship after a smoldering kiss. She attempts to quit seeing Dillon altogether until his truck is stolen and used in a crime, and only she can provide an alibi. As she falls for him, her past with alcoholism taunts her with all the reasons why a future with Dillon won't work. If he refuses to admit to his problem, not even she'll be able to help him, and she won't stick around to watch.

Thank you to the pioneers of independent publishing. Without you, this book wouldn't have made it past the rejection slips. I was already indie publishing but I wanted to check out the traditionally published world with this series. The more I had to defend my work, the more it became mine. I'm proud to share my Midwest farmers and their sometimes too-close-to-home challenges with you. I hope you enjoy this series as much as I love writing it.

For all the latest news, sneak peeks, quarterly short stories, and free material sign up for my newsletter.

CHAPTER 1

$\mathcal{E}$lle Brady tapped a foot against the side of her desk as she studied the insurance statement.

"I got *bills*," she muttered, tossing it to the side. She rubbed her face, a flare of panic burning in her gut.

The "member responsibility" section of her explanation of benefits was absurdly high. She mentally tallied her other bills, including rent and her vehicle payments, and it equaled…not enough. Cutting down on groceries, again, might help, but she needed to buy quality food for her dad or he'd get sick again, and *boom!* More bills.

Her pager vibrated and she sighed, missing the more updated alert system her old job used. She peeked at it. Ah, her next patient. Wait—client. The Moore Mental Health Center insisted on not referring to their customers as patients. In a town as small as Moore, "client" went over better.

Week by week, she'd built her client base since beginning her new job. Her calendar for today was nearly booked. A welcome sight for a paranoid mind that whispered she might never build enough business to hold her job. A full planner meant a full paycheck, and she needed every dime to support her and her dad.

Elle checked the clipboard with her next client's information and oriented herself with his name.

Dillon Walker, a first-time client.

A deep voice radiated through her closed door. "Is there a cube of cheese at the end of this maze?"

The receptionist chuckled. "It takes a while to get use to all the twists and turns."

When the door opened, Elle's gaze landed on the navy-blue ball cap that read "Moore Implement." A tan work jacket stretched across broad shoulders and rugged blue jeans that'd seen better days completed a look that screamed *farmer*. A popular style around Moore, Minnesota.

Eyes as blue as the April sky outside her window stared at her.

She plastered a welcoming smile on her face. "Have a seat, Dillon."

"How're you today, Doc?"

Even though it was a common mistake, she chuckled. "Call me Elle, please. I have a master's in addiction counseling, not a Ph.D. in psychology, so I'm not a doctor."

His voice dropped to a low timbre. "Whatever you want… Elle." He shrugged out of his coat and draped it over the back of his chair.

Whoa. That was almost suggestive. She'd had male clients close to her in age before, but it wasn't common for the person across from her to be interested in anything other than counseling. What was uncommon was her breathless sensation. Ridiculous—she was above that type of reaction to a *client*. She swallowed hard and gathered herself.

As he settled into his seat, she swiveled away from her desk to face him fully.

"So how do we do this?" Dillon's hands rested on his

thighs, but his fingers tapped nonstop. "You ask me questions, I answer?"

His bright gaze swept her body, interest apparent in their depths. Any other room but her office, she'd delight in his attention, but as soon as his name was entered into her schedule…well, off limits was an understatement.

Readying her pen, she prepared to take notes. "Why don't we start by you telling me why you're here?"

His gaze dropped to the floor, his mouth pressed in a firm line. While he formed the right words to explain what brought him into her office, she glanced over at his papers. Twenty-seven. Only a year older than she was. His pause may not be so much about choosing his words, but more about spilling his concerns to a woman his age he'd never met before.

He switched his attention out the window. "My dad wanted me to come."

"Why's that?"

He adjusted his cap. Rearranged it again and finally took it off to reveal a head of reddish-brown hair. "He thought I'd been drinking too much since I came home from the Army."

"But you don't think so?"

One shoulder rolled in a shrug. "I don't think there's anything wrong with having a few beers. I put in long days in the field, long hours helping work the family cattle. Sometimes it's nice to kick back and chill at the end of the night."

Yet, his dad worried about him—and he was here. Since the alcohol question was a little touchy… "You're a farmer?"

"Born and raised," he drawled. "You can't throw a stone in this town and not hit one of us."

Her lips twitched. Truth. The town of ten thousand was surrounded by fields in all four directions. "Do you enjoy it?"

"Other than the weather and seasons dictating my hours,

I'm my own boss—mostly—and I get to drive tractors with tires taller than I am."

I'm my own boss could also mean *I like to be in control.*

Time to test the waters. "Tell me about your history with alcohol, from when you started to why your dad's worried."

"Hell, Doc," he drawled, "it's a small town. Drinking begins in high school around here. Back then, the weekends were spent partying in a field where our parents wouldn't catch us and the cops wouldn't see our cars from the road."

Elle smiled at his nostalgia. So young and carefree. Her high school experience had been anything but. No partying for her. She'd checked groceries and swum her heart out to earn a scholarship. Those two things had been her only hope at getting into a decent college.

"I still find teenagers sometimes," he continued with a laugh, "trying to hide on my land and party. I have the deputy on speed dial."

Small towns and drinking. No wonder Moore could support an addiction counseling center. Not the kind of job security she liked to see, but what an asset for the community. She wished there had been a center around for her parents when she'd been growing up.

And Dillon had just admitted to turning the partying kids in. He didn't join in.

He didn't offer up any more information, so she pressed on. "And what about after high school?"

His expression faded to neutral. "I joined the Army, stayed in for eight years, got out, and came home."

Flat tone. No fidgeting. Dead in the water. He hadn't acted like that type of person, someone who holds himself back, when he'd walked in. Her first impression of him had been the kind of guy that attracted people, helped them open up, not shut down on them.

She switched topics. "Tell me about your dad."

"He died six months ago." Dillon's voice lacked inflection.

Oh… He'd lost a parent, and it was probably the only way he would ever have agreed to book a session with her. "I'm sorry, Dillon."

A noncommittal shrug.

Dillon's emotionless tone didn't speak to his relationship with his father. Was it built on animosity or had they been extremely close? Was he in her office in a belated attempt to repair a father-son relationship, or because they'd been so close, he couldn't *not* do it? She sensed he wasn't ready to open up. "And your mother?"

His face lit up. "She's living in Sioux Falls. After Cash and I came home from the Army, my parents and my aunts and uncles sold the Walker Five to us cousins and retired in style."

"Walker Five?"

He nodded. "I farm with four cousins. That's why I'm only mostly my own boss."

Heaven help the girls of Moore, Minnesota, if the rest of the Walker Five looked as good as Dillon. Four other cousins in the business alone. A big family could offer a lot of support. She considered Dillon. After only a few minutes, she pegged him as the one the others looked up to. Dillon had that appeal, the I'll-take-care-of-you-don't-worry-about-me kind. Elle could've used someone like Dillon in her life.

She jotted down the details. Working with family often came up in her sessions as a trigger point. "Tell me about the Army."

"It was okay."

She waited. Nothing. *Aaand* another tidbit to jot down. "What did you do for work, and where were you stationed?"

"Infantry. I was in Georgia for a few years, Fort Benning. Then went across country to Fort Irwin, California, for the rest." His voice was as bland as when he'd spoken of his dad passing.

So, he closed himself off to emotionally loaded aspects of his life. She jotted that down.

"Any deployments?"

"Iraq. Three of them." A robot would have more inflection.

Just a single deployment brought many current and former military to her office. The odds of three giving Dillon issues he hadn't dealt with yet were high. "Are you concerned about post-traumatic stress disorder?"

Dillon scoffed like PTSD was a mythical creature. It was the biggest reaction she'd gotten from him since he'd walked into her office. "No. I'm not doing anything crazy that'll hit national news."

Elle suppressed a sigh. Typical soldier reaction. "PTSD isn't always dramatic and severe. It can be insidious. Affecting you in small ways at first. Have you been having nightmares, possibly related to your time overseas?"

A muscle tensed in his jaw, but he shook his head. "No."

"Is there anything that happened during your deployment that you want to talk about?"

His expression rivaled granite. "No."

Just once, couldn't it be easy? *Yeah, now that you mention it, I had this awful, nightmare-inducing incident that's haunted me ever since. Let me tell you all about it.*

She could continue asking questions and determine where he shut down, or she could get to the point. "What do you want out of our sessions?"

DILLON CONSIDERED ELLE'S QUESTION. He wanted her number. He wanted to know if she was free Friday night. He wanted to know if he'd ruined his chances with the hot doctor—counselor—by heeding his dad's last request and making this stupid appointment. He'd always been attracted to intelligent women, but her soft-spoken persona, the way she considered his words but hadn't pressed further… appealed to him in a way that surprised him.

"We have five rounds together," he finally answered, "you tell me what goes on."

"Well, it depends. Usually when someone comes to me, they're ready to work on their recovery or face the reasons behind their addiction." She shifted in her seat, uncrossed her leg and crossed the other one. He glimpsed a knee between the top of her boots and the hem of her skirt. "What are you here for?"

Good fucking question. His head hurt because he'd been sleeping like shit. He had a tractor calling his name and a field that needed plowing.

He glanced around the room. Was it too much to ask for a clock? How rude would it be to pull out his phone to look at the time? As much as he wanted to stay just to be in Elle's fresh apple pie-smelling office, watching that lone tendril of flaxen hair caress her cheek, his foot started tapping.

"I'm not here because I'm an alcoholic. Honestly, Doc, I feel like I'm wasting your time."

Understanding lit her emerald eyes. "You were close to your dad."

He blew out a breath. How'd she interpret that from what he said? "Yeah."

"And he was worried about you? Why?"

Dillon spread his hands. "I'm guessing because I kept my beer in his fridge. He wasn't a big drinker so anything I drank looked like a lot to him."

Scratch, scratch. She jotted down notes. "How much do you drink?"

"Couple of beers here and there." He smirked because

seriously, it was a normal amount. Giving in, he pulled out his phone and checked the time. Good God, hardly any time had passed. "Sorry to cut and run on ya, but I gotta get going."

Her brows lifted, surprise in her eyes. "You have your next appointment set up?"

"Yep, all four of them." *That I plan to cancel on my way out the door.* "See you next time."

Geez, he hated feeling rude, especially to a sweet-smelling goddess with a smile that made him want to talk about things he worked so hard to ignore.

"Okay." She appeared to recover from his announcement that he was leaving. "For next time, I'd like you to think about what you're feeling when you have a drink."

Dillon threw his cap on and stood. She was still talking so he didn't want to completely run out on her, but that's what his feet were telling him they wanted to do.

"Just general emotions." She rose with him. "If you have something more specific, like an event, a conversation, that'd be great."

"Got it." He gave her the smile he used on his gram when she hounded him about his lack of sleep. "See ya, Friday."

"Bye, Dillon."

He sensed her following him to the door. When he stepped into the hallway, he stopped, a moment of panic spiked. For fuck's sake, how did he get out of this place?

"Take the first left and then a right and you'll the see the waiting room sign."

"Got it." He mentally scowled at himself. A day that started out as pure crap disintegrated to downright humiliating. He could barely string more than a few words together to talk to her and he was lost in the damn hallway. To save face, he shot her another charming smile over his shoulder. "See you Friday, Elle."

As he turned away to walk down the hall, the image of her was seared into his consciousness. He'd chosen Elle after cruising the clinic's website and reading in her bio that she was new to town. Perfect, he'd thought at the time, she didn't know him and hadn't grown up with any of his family. While her professional photo had shown a pretty lady, the real Elle Brady knocked his socks off.

No way was he going in there four more times. He didn't want to see professional concern in her gaze, he wanted to see interest. She was a good-looking woman around his age. He didn't want to cry on her shoulder—not that he had anything to sob about. They should be flirting, making plans for a date…normal shit. Not this therapy bullshit.

Yet he breezed past the receptionist desk without canceling his appointments. The drive to see her again too strong. Just one more time. He'd cancel after the second session. Ugh. But she'd asked him to do some thinking before then.

Fine. She asked him to think about what was going on in his noggin when he had a beer. Now, he could guarantee that all he'd think about was her.

CHAPTER 2

Clicking her office door shut, Elle turned but stood stock still. Dillon had left the office, but he hadn't left her mind. *Come on.* She'd been around handsome men before. Dillon's keen blue eyes and air of responsibility shouldn't have wormed their way past her guards—for so many reasons beyond him being her client. She wasn't foolish, she wasn't impulsive, she wasn't one to fall for a man with strong, broad shoulders that could carry her through a fire.

She wasn't like that and she'd prove it to herself during his next session. Three more days and he'd be back. Maybe. She wouldn't be surprised if he cancelled.

Part of her would be relieved. Not that he cancelled his appointment, but that he was done with her as a client. Her heart fluttered, her stomach had butterflies. Her female personality threatened to override her professional one.

Chewing on her lip, she walked to her desk. Not a good way to start off a new job. Her probation period was nearly over and she'd get a raise. She *needed* a raise. What if Dillon didn't cancel? What if she'd developed an—ugh, she hated even thinking of the possibility—infatuation that could affect his care? Could she discretely transfer his care to another counselor?

She snorted. No. A twenty-something single woman transferring her twenty-something single—was he?—client. What else would it look like? She could use the excuse he was adamant he wasn't battling an addiction. But that might demean her abilities in front of her boss. She was still on probation and transferring Dillon might affect the raise she'd earn after her probationary period.

If he wasn't now, he surely would be. Evasive and proud, yet much like an iceberg. She'd caught glimpses of his inner turmoil and had no doubt that he handled whatever was stressing him poorly.

Those baby blues of his. And that smile.

Yes. Oh God, should she transfer his care? She didn't want him to be discouraged. No, no. Four sessions. She could handle four sessions.

A knock on her door brought her upright. "Yes?"

Betsy, the short, round children's counselor scurried in. "Did I just see Dillon Walker leave?"

Elle opened her mouth to answer, but Betsy held up her hand, silencing her. "No, wait." Betsy sniffed. "I can smell him. He was here. Do you think that's aftershave, or cologne, or just a natural fragrance all the Walker boys put off to make the ladies want to throw their bras at them?"

Elle burst out laughing. "Betsy!" Ever since she started months ago, Betsy had welcomed her with her vibrant personality and toeing-the-line comments. Around her, Elle felt more like the one in her forties instead of Betsy.

"I'm happily married, but I'm not dead and I like to look at anyone under forty with the last name Walker."

"I'm afraid I haven't met the others."

Betsy plopped in the seat Dillon had vacated. "Too bad we

have the conflict of interest issue. I would've recommended him for you. He's a solid guy, good morals, works hard. They all do—work hard. The good morals doesn't apply to his cousin Cash."

"Oh?"

"Mmm-hmm. Yeah. Tom cat. Not Dillon, though. He's the oldest of all of them. Surprised to see him here, actually."

I think he was weirded out seeing himself here. Elle wanted so badly to comment on Dillon, ask questions, but unlike Betsy, she feared for her job. But she did note that he was the oldest on his chart. If they were that close, then perhaps he'd taken on the Type A personality of an oldest child.

"I have someone coming in five minutes." She tipped her head back, eyes closed. "Your office smells so damn good. Where do you get those candles?"

"When I went back to Minneapolis last month, I stocked up. Seems to relax the clients."

"Working on me," she mumbled. Her lids flipped open. "Want to go to lunch later?"

Lunch would be awesome. Someday she'd like to be free to dedicate her lunches to eating. "I can't. I have to run home."

Betsy's expression softened. "I forgot your dad lives with you. At least in Moore, you're five minutes from anywhere. Why don't you stop by after you check on him?"

"I usually eat with Dad and leave instructions for heating up dinner. Dad's been so frail since his chemo, I don't want him toddling around the kitchen when I'm not there. Thanks for the offer. Please don't stop asking." With a sinking feeling in her gut, she knew they'd give up on her eventually. She'd been turning down invitations since before high school in order to take care of her dad.

"The offer's always open." Betsy sashayed back to her own office.

Elle drew a deep breath. Betsy was right. Dillon had left his own masculine scent in her office.

Gotta get him out of my mind.

Regardless of the conflict of interest, she wasn't going to start something with an alcoholic. Not when she'd been going home to one her whole life.

CHAPTER 3

The bright sun of an early spring sky shone down on the dirt road Dillon ambled down in his signature red Case IH tractor. Eight black wheels, all taller than he was, carried him away from the field he'd been plowing after a long, harsh winter. Glancing in the rearview mirror revealed half a field with rich soil where foliage from last year's harvest had been churned under by chisel plow.

He should be back there plowing the other half. Dried and withered corn stalks from last year's yield could be left until planting. No-till they called it, better for cost and the environment by increasing water and organic material retention, but Dillon wanted a light plow before April showers washed tons of corn debris into the lake nearby.

He took a swig from his water bottle. If only it held something stronger than H_2O. The giant rumbling beast may not be decked out with all the high-tech gadgets installed in the new tractors, but at least he could sit in a cozy cab, out of the cool spring wind that blew fierce across the prairie-turned-farmland of western Minnesota.

He pulled his cell phone out of his pocket to dial the farm's mechanic, his cousin Brock.

"Hey, tractor whisperer, engine's running hot," Dillon snapped, releasing pent-up irritation that he had to abandon plowing on a—finally—nice day. "It's running low on coolant."

"Can you limp her back to your shop?" Brock asked in his signature calm manner.

"I emptied most of my water bottle in the coolant tank, after I waited *forever* for it to cool enough so I could touch it." Could've been worse. Waiting an hour in the dirt in Moore was better than the blistering, sandy desert of Iraq. More pleasant and he didn't get sand caked on his balls. "I'll take it slow. If it's not pulling the plow, it should last."

"I'm on my way back from town. My tools are in the back of my truck. Get it to the shop and I'll take a look at it." Brock disconnected.

His first time getting out to work after a rough winter. He'd rushed it, gambling on the weather, wanting to prove…something.

If only the tractor were fine, he'd be done and showing his family he was just fine, too.

Three miles to go. He rolled along, bumping gently over the washboard gouges left in the gravel. Dillon didn't push it. Shut everything down that didn't need to be running. A beautiful day for the time of year, it'd still be a chilly walk if the engine overheated and he had to leave the cab of the tractor. He didn't have the time—he had an appointment to get to.

With Elle.

He calculated it'd take another ten minutes to finish the remaining distance back to his place. The roads were still a little muddy in areas from the spring thaw. Instead of swerving to miss the major wet spots and ride the ditches, he kept the metal beast lumbering straight and forward, unwilling to chance anything giving it the hiccup that would stop the engine altogether.

After he crested one of the gently rolling hills in the long stretch of road, the copse of trees surrounding his home came into view. The only break in them allowed the long driveway off the main gravel road to run through into his yard. He liked the privacy.

Brock leaned against the tailgate of his grimy Ford F350 parked by the garage attached to the house. From the way the vehicle looked, Brock's ass was likely brown and dirty from touching it and he wouldn't care. He rarely wore good clothes—if he had any.

Brock trotted across the yard to the shop and pushed the big door open. Dillon idled inside. He'd made it. He killed the engine and rolled his neck to release the tension.

He could really use a drink.

Not that he'd mention that to anyone. The worried looks his family exchanged behind his back weren't as concealed as they'd intended. They didn't understand. Dillon had left for the Army at eighteen. They weren't used to him being legally old enough to drink.

A shitty day before noon warranted a cool drink to relax.

Dillon climbed down the narrow ladder from the cab, ignoring stiffened muscles from the stressful drive. Brock scaled the side of the tractor and lifted the hood.

Dillon checked his watch. "Hey, man. I've gotta go."

Brock popped his head out, black baseball hat turned backward. "There has to be a leak. I'll find it, but I doubt I'll get it fixed today."

"Damn. I wanted to get the northeast section done before the rain they're forecasting shows up."

"It's early spring, we've got time." Brock continued his engine inspection.

Ugh, that's what they'd all been saying. Dillon's opinion of the weather was: Wouldn't it be really handy to have the blasted fields plowed *before* Mother Nature sprung a late season blizzard on them? Ultimately, the weather had the final say in everything they did. Instead of coasting, Dillon wanted to get shit done.

He trotted to his truck. Nothing more was going to be accomplished today. After his appointment, he'd grab some oil for his pickup. He'd gotten the reminder text from Brock that his pickup was due. If Dillon didn't open a window of time, Brock would continue texting and calling, repeat.

All the way to town, he thought about Elle. Glancing in the rearview mirror, he turned his face back and forth. No grease or dirt. Checking out his clothing, he groaned. Not so with his jeans and plaid button-up.

For the last appointment, he'd showered before, unwilling to show up looking like a drunk fuck in ratty, wrinkled clothing. Well…he checked himself one more time. He looked like he'd been working, not holed up in a bottle.

One more look in the mirror. Good. His eyes were no longer bloodshot.

ELLE ARRANGED the pamphlet and business card on her desk. Rearranged them, straightened them so they were side by side.

Her pager buzzed. Oh, thank goodness. The wait was killing her. She'd had a full morning, but the hour before Dillon's slot had been empty. Longest sixty minutes ever.

Voices drifted through her door.

"Thank you, ma'am."

Elle closed her eyes. His baritone hadn't changed. By the

time the door opened, she donned her competent counselor mask.

His smile of greeting and the way his eyes locked onto her kept her plastered in her chair. He was lethal. Owned his own business, attractive and charming, and a—former—military guy. She felt bad for the woman he set his sights on.

Betsy popped her head in. "I delivered him safely. He almost talked Miss Debra into letting him come back himself. I said I still get lost in this place."

Dillon chuckled. "I tried to run for it, but she's a tenacious one."

"Carving those words on my gravestone," Betsy sang as she left and shut the door behind her.

Still laughing, he swaggered to the chair her clients usually sat in. Not as…clean…as his previous session, but the look fit him. Too well.

No jacket today, instead the long-sleeved gray and green flannel covered his muscular frame, and not that she cared, but she might have to wipe off the seat before her next client.

She could use his appearance and open with a neutral topic. "How was work?"

"Unfinished." He whipped his hat off and hung it on his knee as he riffled through his hair with his other hand. Hat head shouldn't be a worry for him with his hair trimmed so short.

"Because you had to stop for the appointment?"

His brows raised. "No, it's not you. My tractor broke down. I can't get back into the fields. Maybe not even this weekend if Brock needs a part. And look at that sky."

"Pretty frustrating."

"Yeah," he snorted.

"What do you do when a tractor breaks down?"

The break in his schedule obviously bothered him.

"Fix in place or lug it back home if it can move. I keep a

tool kit in the cab, but that's not always enough. Then Brock'll come out with the truck. If he can't fix it, then we have to get someone out." His hands rubbed up and down his thighs and he randomly tapped his heels.

Elle tilted her head. Good thing she'd asked about work. "What if the mechanic can't fix it?"

He clenched and unclenched his fists. "Then we'll have to upgrade and Brock won't be able to touch it if we have problems. Part of the contract." He gave the last words air quotes.

"You can't repair your own equipment?"

"Nope. So many electronics, not that my cousin couldn't figure out much of it, but the tractor dealers got us by the balls."

She scribbled a few notes.

"Doc, are you writing down that the tractor guy has got me by the balls?"

A laugh sputtered out and her last word was illegible. "Not word for word, no. A new tractor would be expensive, correct?"

He waved it off. "Yeah, but the farm can cover it. Our uncles followed Gramps's motto: A farm that spends all its money can't be profitable. Me and the boys follow the same guidelines. I even have it as the header under Walker Five on all our paperwork."

"How much would a new tractor cost?"

He shifted in his seat and his fingers tapped along the arm rest. "I don't know, two or two-fifty."

Comprehending the numbers was difficult until she added zeros. *"Two hundred thousand?"*

His good-natured smile kept her from feeling naïve. "Depends if we go new or used. I've seen used Magnums go for less than two hundred, but the newer ones with the tracks are probably way more."

Spending that kind of money would stress a person out. "Did you think on what we talked about at our last session?"

His expression drained to neutral. Suddenly, she missed his easy grin.

"I'm telling you, the only thing I'm thinking about is that I want to relax."

"Are there any things that can help you relax other than a drink?"

He cocked an arrogant eyebrow. Her cheeks warmed as a flush flooded her skin.

She cleared her throat and crossed her leg to prop her clipboard on it, like a shield from his intensity. "Do you drink at the end of the day, or throughout?"

"I'm not an alcoholic. I don't nurse a beer all day, just have a couple before bed."

"At night, we're looking for soothing, but not stimulating, activities for you." Damn her blush. This never felt awkward with other clients. "A long shower, reading…do you know of any others?"

"Sorry, to disappoint you, Elle. I get in late, heat up supper, and hit the hay."

"Do you have nightmares?"

His slight recoil and clenched jaw spoke volumes. "Nothing I can't handle."

"Tell me about the Army."

He shrugged as if brushing off the entirety of his military experience. "Eight years in, then we got out."

Wait… "We?"

His eyes flared. Busted. "My cousin Cash joined when I did, got out when I did."

"You two were close then?"

He nodded, his features strained. "We were."

She waited. Nothing. "Why'd you get out, Dillon?"

"I came home to farm. End of story."

Or was it the beginning? They were interrupted by a phone vibrating. She frowned. It wasn't hers.

He ignored it. "Sorry, I gotta cut this short again. Need to take advantage of being in town when the businesses are open."

His phone fell silent and she swallowed the lump in her throat. "Okay, for next time," she snagged the two items from her desk, "I'd like to refer you to a colleague of mine. I think he'll be a good fit for you, and, if you'd like, I can fill him in—"

"No way." He sat forward, his expression startled. "No, no one else."

"Dillon, I don't think I'm the counselor you need."

He shook his head, adamant. "Elle," his gaze captured hers, "I only came back because I wanted to see you again."

She sighed. "Because you wanted to see me again as a counselor, or as a woman?" If he'd come back for personal reasons, she be flattered. Totally, unprofessionally, pleased. She willed him to give the right answer. That he viewed her as his counselor.

He cocked his head at her. "I'm not an alcoholic. I see you as a woman."

Her heart sank. "And that's why I can no longer help you. I'm sorry, Dillon. Ethically, it isn't right."

His phone vibrated again, and again he ignored it. "I'm not seeing anyone else. Last time I was here, I planned to cancel. I *only* came back because of you."

For the first time, she cursed that he'd booked an appointment with her. A handsome man with an admirable job was interested and he was as far off limits as could be.

"Phil is an excellent addiction counselor and I really think you need to explore any issues that cause you to drink."

He spoke in a low tone. "I'm not coming back if I can't see you again. I mean it, Elle. Phil Fresnick graduated with my mom. I'm not sitting in his office knowing he took her to prom."

Ah yes. A common issue in small town mental health. Overlapping relationships beyond counselor/client. Yet, Phil had made it work. He had to be nearing retirement.

"What about—"

"I know them all, maybe not personally but we're all connected. Why do you think I ended up in your office?" His phone vibrated again. "You know what, I'm sorry, Elle." His tone wasn't hostile, but startled her with its tenderness. "I've put you in a bad position. I've said over and over that I don't need to be here. I'm going to cancel my remaining appointments, don't worry about it. I feel crappy taking up a slot when someone who's really sick can use it."

Her heart sank at not being able to see him again, but transferring his care was the right thing to do on her end. She couldn't give up on him, though. He was hurting and he wouldn't admit it.

"I really want to encourage you to find someone you're comfortable with, perhaps attend an Alcoholics Anonymous meeting to try it out."

He scoffed. "Nothing anonymous in this town."

"There's Fargo an hour away. Sioux Falls is two."

Again, his phone went off. He growled and pulled it out of his pocket only to scowl at the screen.

"I'll think about it. I have to go take this. See ya around?"

Why did his words sound like he'd asked her on a date? When he walked out, she tossed the clipboard on her desk.

Well, that was end of her and Dillon Walker.

"WHAT'S UP?" Dillon kept his voice in check. He was the oldest, the guys still looked to him as the ultimate authority.

So if Brock lit up his phone to no end, it had to be something important.

"First off, what the fuck are you doing with a six pack in the cab?"

"What the hell are you talking about?" Dillon hissed to keep his voice from carrying into the other offices.

"I cleaned out your lunch bag, thinking it had to go in the fridge before the food went bad."

"You called me about some completely full cans that I haven't drunk?"

"Not one or two. Shit, Dillon. 'Don't drink and drive' goes for tractors, too."

Dillon bit down on the inside of his cheek. He was the calm, reasonable one, he had to damn well act like it. "You think I don't know that? I owe Aaron a sixer and figured I could pay up if he stopped out to talk. I was plowing the quarter by his house, you know."

Brock fell silent.

He pushed on before Brock could question him. "You said first thing, what else?"

His heart thumped as he waited for Brock. Was he going to turn into an old hen and cluck about the fridge full of beer? Because Dillon didn't like to make a ton of piddly trips into town. Might as well buy bulk if the stores carried it.

"I think the coolant tank was punctured."

Dillon waved at the receptionist as he walked out. Hopefully, Elle would cancel his appointments. He wasn't going to sit on the phone while they tried to talk him into rescheduling with someone else. "How?"

"Exactly. I can't figure it out. The only thing I can think of is someone tampered with it."

CHAPTER 4

Grateful the workday was done, Elle drove home. Dillon consumed her thoughts for the few minutes it took to get to her house. She'd messed up. Had there been another way? Could she have kept counseling him and continued to be professional? He'd said himself he'd only come to see her.

No. She wasn't responsible for coaxing him into Moore Mental Health. That was up to him. Just like it was up to her to quit thinking about him and move on.

She would've laughed at the unfairness, but life hadn't been fair to her before, so why would it start now? She approached her little square home and pulled into the garage. Then took a few moments for impromptu meditation. Most days she loved her job. Some days it reminded her of all the reasons why she'd gone into the mental health field, specifically addiction counseling. On those days, she required more self-care than usual before she went in to take care of her original patient, a man who'd danced off the twelve steps more often than he'd followed them. After supper, she'd soak in a warm, sudsy bath.

Her stomach growled, interrupting her zen. The lasagna she'd asked her dad to throw in the oven sounded heavenly.

When she entered the house, no delicious scents of cheesy, meaty goodness basking in oregano greeted her. Dinner should've been done by now, warmth filling the kitchen from an hour and a half of baking. Her father was nowhere to be seen.

"Dad?"

A strangled noise echoed from deep within the house. Elle dropped her purse and followed the sound. Damn it, she'd checked on him at noon and he'd been fine. Assured her he'd be okay to throw the meal in.

"Dad?"

He called to her again, sounding tired and in pain. Rushing through the house, she bee-lined for the door to the basement. Her heart bottomed to her toes.

No, no, no.

He lay at the bottom. His feet rested higher on a couple of stairs with his body draped onto the floor.

"Dad!"

She flew down the steps while digging out her phone.

"Ellie," he rasped weakly, "just help me up. I'll be fine."

"How far did you fall? What were you doing down here?" She stepped around him to kneel on the floor.

"I was," he stopped to take a wheezy breath, "getting the lasagna to put in the oven."

"It was in the fridge, ready to go. Don't you remember me telling you that?" Why was she chewing him out? He'd been injured badly, his normally weak frame crumpled in a painful heap. "Where do you hurt?" She dialed 9-1-1.

"I'm fine," he continued to argue, his wiry form seeking a more comfortable position. His face screwed up in agony.

"No, you're not. You probably broke a hip." Speaking rapidly into the phone, she described her dad's predicament, where the majority of his pain was, and what she could tell eyeballing his breathing and color.

After she hung up, time gradually ticked by while they waited for the ambulance to arrive.

SUNLIGHT PUMMELED DILLON'S HEAD. With a deep groan, he rolled over and forced himself to sit up. If he went back to sleep to escape the tortuous light, he'd hear crap from his cousins when he showed up late. He couldn't deal with the cryptic comments when they found out he'd been working in his shop past midnight because he'd slept in until noon. It was like his grandma's nosy friends lived around him.

Dillon rubbed his eyes and scanned the room. No wonder the sun was so damn bright. He'd fallen asleep on the couch again. The curtains covering the large picture window in the living room where he'd fallen asleep were tied to the sides.

He shoved to his feet, wobbled a little. Plodding his way to the bathroom, he kicked into a pile of empty aluminum cans, sending them clanking across the floor. Around him were more than a half dozen silver beer cans glinting in the light.

Funny, he thought he'd only had a couple. Maybe a few were from the night before; he didn't remember cleaning them up.

As the shower warmed, he rubbed his eyes and recalled Brock's discovery. Dillon had told him to table the suspicion until they could prove it. He trusted his family and there was no use getting rumors started. They blew through town faster than prairie winds.

The shower served to help him feel both refreshed and like pounded dog shit, courtesy of his night on the couch. He dressed and went in search of water and nutrition, other than the liquid barley he'd ingested the previous night.

He rummaged through the fridge and withdrew a baggie of his mom's meatloaf. Not one for ceremony, he stood over the sink and ate the leftover goodness. It was better than sitting at the table across from nothing, with only the wall to look at. And thanks to Mama, he was never short of quality food. She stocked his freezer with meals since she thought he'd get nothing else if it wasn't from a can. Each time, he reminded her he manned a mean grill, that ranchers were always stocked with steak, but he didn't argue too hard. She missed cooking for her family and her meals were fantastic.

Because he didn't feel awful enough, his thoughts returned once again to Elle. All night, he'd cursed himself for ever agreeing to counseling.

Sorry, Dad, gave it a shot, but you were worried for nothing.

And next time his mom came to visit from Sioux Falls, Dillon could tell her, yep, he'd done it.

Did he have a chance with Elle, or would she always see him as an off-limits client?

A question he'd asked himself for hours last night. He gave up on his therapy, but he hadn't given up on her. A woman like her… She was one of a kind. He admired the hell out of the fact that she'd stuck to a decision that he'd rebelled against, all because she'd been adamant it was the right thing to do. Their counselor/client relationship was over, but he didn't want that to be the end of him and Elle.

He shook his head. Might as well move onto something he had a little power over.

His mind rolled through the chores to be done. The ground was wet from a sprinkling of midnight rain that the sun was already evaporating. Good, after Brock fixed the tractor he could get back out plowing.

He leaned forward. Were those footprints? He squinted.

Yes, there were muddy footprints around the door of his shop. Maybe Brock had come early to work on the tractor. He glanced at the clock.

No, Brock said he had to wait until the parts store opened at nine today so he could pick some items up first. The store only opened five minutes ago. Dillon stared at the concrete flat poured in front of the shop. Meant to catch big chunks of mud and muck before rolling equipment inside, it caught the muddy footprints of Dillon's mystery visitor.

Dillon grabbed his hat and jacket and headed to the shop. The footprints went through the door. Dammit, they never locked anything. There'd been no need to. Following the footprints from the building, he determined the returning prints from where they smudged the first set.

Whoever it was arrived after it rained while Dillon slept on the couch. He examined his lawn and spied the patch his visitor had run through to get his shoes all dirty. The caller must've stuck to the squishy greenery that bordered the driveway and stepped in the wet, soggy flowerbed his mother used to grow her petunias in.

Dillon smiled grimly to himself. Those beds hadn't seen a flower in two years, but he'd tilled them. Eventually, his mother would get sick of seeing empty black soil when she visited and plant annuals for him. Good thing he hadn't let it grow over, or there might not have been prints.

He walked up his drive, staying parallel with the tracks, and reached the main road. In the stretch of gravel, there were a few sets of fresh tire marks, but nothing unusual, until he spotted a grouping of tracks on the side of the road. Either his unexpected visitor didn't know wet gravel roads held onto their history longer than pavement or didn't care that when the dirt dried, vehicle impressions lingered.

He inspected the area. Sure as shit, it looked like a car had been parked there. He walked around the tracks gathering as much information as possible. One set of prints, one visitor. Intruder. A visitor wouldn't park on the road and break into his shop in the middle of the night.

Shit. His shop—where all his tools were. All his *expensive* tools.

He trotted back, but pulled to a stop before he charged inside. His instinct to radio in information and bring his weapon up to the ready hit him hard.

He shook his head. This wasn't fucking Iraq and he didn't have a group of soldiers to pass orders to. The only radio he had was the standard one in his truck that he listened to music on.

Still, he couldn't shake the wish that he had a gun. No, his hunting rifle would stay tucked away in the gun safe. Using that to clear his shop when he was reasonably sure his intruder was long gone fulfilled all the fantasies of the PTSD whisperers.

He was no longer a soldier, so he'd do what a normal dude would do, like call the cops. First, he texted his cousins and asked if any of them stopped out late last night. Next, he used the camera on his phone to take pictures of the area around the door and the concrete where the prints were the most visible.

Entering the building, he purposefully strode in like he didn't have a care in the world. He flipped on all of the overhead lights, ignoring the spike in adrenaline that sent his heart racing. The action of stepping into a dark building with a hint of danger assaulted his brain with memories. The rustle of boots and gear creaking as crouched forms broke off into various rooms. Just like that, he was back in the desert with sweat pouring down his back and his helmet jostling on his head as his team swept through building after building.

Dillon's focus blurred. He shook his head and forced his

gaze back to the floor. He lost sense of where the tracks led, but squatting down he detected the prints. Inspecting the floor, he worked his way toward the workbench.

His stuff had been moved. Dillon had mentored under his uptight father all his life. Every gadget had a place. They weren't thrown back on the bench or tossed into the standing toolbox where he'd have to sift through them to find the one he needed. They were lined up by size and organized by type and he never put away filthy tools.

He made a mental note of the disrupted tools while he took more pictures. They may not be good for the cops, but he and Brock could determine if something was missing. It didn't appear anything was stolen, but then why would someone break in?

Had the tractor really been tampered with?

He made a quick sweep of the shop. The tractor they used for plowing and haying was parked and waiting for its repairs. Next to it, the smaller tractor with its snow-blower and bucket attachments sat with the riding lawn mower that looked miniature in comparison to the others.

His phone pinged with text replies of *no, but on my way*; *fuck no, some of us have to work today*; and *why, miss me?* Nothing yet from Cash who was probably extracting himself from a girl's bed without waking her because then he'd have to pretend he remembered her name.

The familiar rumble of Brock's massive truck snatched his attention. Dillon jogged out to meet him. He sidestepped the footprints drying on the concrete and waited for Brock to park and get out.

"What's up with the text?" Brock asked, grabbing some boxes from the bed of his truck.

Dillon motioned for him to follow. "Someone came out here in the middle of the night. They were in here going through my shit."

His cousin dumped the boxes by the plowing tractor's engine. "Anything stolen?"

Dillon hadn't expected Brock to get worked up. Brock would be more likely to get worked up because the intruder interfered with his workday.

"Not that I can tell."

Brock took his black Ford racing hat off and scratched his head. It was a move Dillon had watched his uncle, Brock's dad, do constantly when he was standing over one of his collector Mustangs. "I knew it."

"Someone punched a hole in our coolant tank." Why mess with an old tractor? "I'll check the equipment while you work on fixing the tractor."

Brock put his hat on backward and started emptying the boxes.

They had no enemies. If this were Cash's place, he'd suspect a jealous boyfriend or ex of one of his cousin's many hook-ups. But Dillon spent his time working and any one-night stands were deliberately with the female versions of Cash. And the last one was...it'd been a while, and last he heard, she'd met a new guy and moved in with him. No names of grudge holders came to mind.

If inconvenience had been the goal, it wouldn't take a farming genius to figure out which tractor got used the most in the fields. They relied on it in the spring when the snow melted and the ground thawed to work the fields for planting by the middle of May.

This time of year, they used many of their tractor attachments. Dillon went outside where they were lined up. A quick scan revealed nothing obviously wrong. Dillon checked the plow. He inspected all the bolts and hydraulics carefully. And then he saw it.

The reality of their situation crashed down on him. "Hey, Brock. C'mere."

He heard a clang and a muffled, "Gimme a minute."

While waiting, Dillon checked the rest of the equipment, but found nothing else. By the time he finished, Brock waited by the old disc harrow they never used since the no-till method took over.

"Come here and check out the attachment points for the blades."

It didn't take Brock more than a minute to find the problem. "Son of a bitch. You wouldn't have known until you got all the way out there and tried to use it. The hydraulics would've failed."

"Yep. How much do you want to bet whoever did this didn't know we don't use it anymore? We only went no-till last year. I'll call the police to make a report. Think you can fix the coolant tank and still give me time to get out there and finish the northeast section?"

"It'll be a quick fix, but I'll wait until law enforcement gets what they need."

"We'll need to start locking our houses and all the other buildings." Brock's eyes widened in alarm. Dillon surmised why. "Do you know where your keys are at?"

"I'll find them," Brock grumbled. "Nobody's getting in my shop and touching my 'Stangs."

CHAPTER 5

*D*illon rubbed his aching temples as he walked down the long, stark hallway. It'd been another night on the couch and he was paying for it. Why did the nursing home lights have to be so bright?

At least Sunday was traditionally a sleep-in day so the clock reading eleven didn't give him a heart attack when he woke. He blamed the dreams filled with sand, shadows flitting through adobe buildings, and the explosions startling enough to wake him up. Over a week they'd been raging, thanks to the break-in. His head thudded with each step and the two full glasses of water he'd downed did nothing for the cotton mouth he'd woken up with.

Nodding to one of the CNAs his grandma claimed was her favorite, he stepped into a room. Gram sat in an overstuffed chair, staring out the window.

"Gram, how ya doing?"

He relished the change of smells. From blah and sterile, to warm and cinnamon. The scent conjured images of him as a boy, running in for a piece of her scrumptious apple pie.

"Dillon, what a surprise."

His wrinkled, little grandma always said that even though he'd been stopping in every Sunday since he'd been home. He leaned down to kiss her soft forehead before collapsing in a chair.

"Tough weekend?" She pinned him with a knowing look. Like she knew it wasn't the work kicking his butt, but the after-work fun. She oughta know, raising five boys.

"Same as always," he replied.

Sad but true. Him and a ton of work he couldn't get to that left him with too much damn time on his hands. At least they'd gotten cable television out on the farm after he'd left for basic training. It made the quiet nights a little less barren when he could watch something other than his redundant DVD collection. It was a nice change from the hours of the radio while he was in the tractor cab.

"How are the fields looking?"

Gram loved talking shop. She'd had her hand in as much of the outdoor work as the indoor "woman's work." He doubted his grandfather would've been able to grow their farming operation as much as he had if he hadn't married Gram. Her drive and ambition, and his grandpa's inclination to make Gram happy, made it an operation envied in the tri-county area. And that was back when it was Walker One. Five kids and several major technological advances later, they'd been able to work much more of the land.

"The fields look like black gold, Gram."

She grinned, her teeth too big for her mouth, but she insisted on wearing her dentures because she'd paid good money to have them made. "I suppose you haven't gotten out in them yet?"

"Nah. It warmed up so early this year, I started plowing last week." The others might give him shit for jumping the weather gun, but Gram would understand.

She shrugged one bony shoulder. "We might get a cold

snap coming through, or one of those polar vortexes, but plowing now won't hurt anything. What are you planting this year?"

"The wheat prices are still down, so we'll go with sunflowers and canola. Aaron has part of his land in CRP."

"Bah, the land is hearty. Farm smart and you don't need any conservation reserve program bossing you around."

She said the same thing every year. To her, farming smart meant treating the hell out of the land with pesticides, herbicides, and fertilizers to get the most out of each crop.

"We're humoring the government, Gram."

A bad year in farming hit the pocket book pretty hard, so he and his cousins utilized every resource and program out there to maximize crops without stripping the earth. To them, CRP was money they earned for doing nothing except expending their resources on another aspect of their business.

"The government will change their minds next year." Gram nodded in agreement.

"Keeping it exciting in here?"

She sported her toothy smile. "I do enjoy the birds. That wall-to-wall cage in the entertainment area sure is something. And they play Lawrence Welk every once in a while. An elementary school stopped to visit and give us Easter baskets." She narrowed her gaze on him. "It was wonderful, since I haven't any great-grandchildren running around."

Dillon shifted in his seat. He sincerely hoped all of his cousins endured the same discomfort when they visited Gram. Or was it his due? "I'm only twenty-seven."

"I had all five kids, four of them out of diapers, by the time I was your age. And that was after a late start."

"Good thing Gramps tamed you in time." His grandpa used to joke he'd won over Gram only because she was desperate.

Gram chortled. Her body may be weak and frail, but her mind was sharp and she didn't offend easily. He looked forward to Sundays.

Her smile died and she sighed. "Well, he did what another couldn't."

Dillon cocked his head about to ask what she meant when a familiar voice in the hallway caught his attention.

Of all places, what was she doing here?

Elle walked by with the nursing home director, turning her head in time to catch his eye. Surprise registered on her face, but her attention went back to the lady next to her.

Before he thought it through, he was up and rushing out the door. "I'll be right back."

He could've swore his grandma said, "Go get her," before he rushed out of the room.

"Hey, Elle." Dillon jogged to catch up with her.

The director and Elle stopped to wait for him.

Elle halfheartedly smiled, like she didn't know if she should acknowledge she knew him. "What are you doing here, Dillon?"

Anne answered for him, a huge smile stretched across her face. "Dillon Walker's a familiar face around here."

"I hang with my grandma on Sundays," he explained. "What are you doing here?"

"I'm researching the facility for a family member. Anne was kind enough to meet with me for a tour today instead of trying to find a time during the week around my schedule."

Dillon latched on to a way to get Elle alone. "When you're done with Anne, why don't you stop by and interview a resident? Gram will tell it like it is."

Anne chuckled. "That she will. Agnes Walker won't hold back."

Elle's smile was the same he'd see in her office. "Thank you, but I don't—"

"Oh, what an offer, thank you," Anne talked over her. "We'll only be a few more minutes."

Elle blinked and glanced at him as Anne tugged her away. Getting to know Elle Brady would be an uphill battle, but his gut told him to keep trying.

Her hips swayed in worn blue jeans. A maroon Minnesota Gophers sweatshirt and Nikes looked as good on her as her skirts and blouses. Her hair hung loose and wavy, not in the sleek straightened style she'd worn at their last appointment.

He liked the casual look.

He wandered back into Gram's room.

"Where is she?"

Damn, Gram was sharp.

"She might have a family member moving in here. Anne's giving her a tour, then I invited her back here to interview you."

Gram nodded in understanding. "That'll work."

How many guys could claim their grandma was their wingman?

They chatted about the weather. She reminisced, all stories he'd heard for the last twenty years. He filled her in on the repairs Brock did for him. He left out the vandalisms and how they began locking the doors. If she heard from someone else first, he'd catch hell. So would all his cousins. Still, the risk was worth not worrying her.

More time ticked by.

Elle wasn't going to show. The first woman he'd met in years who made him think maybe coming home to an empty house wasn't his only future and he'd fucked it up before he'd even met her.

Yeah, I need to set up five sessions with Elle Brady.

A soft tap at the door cut Gram off mid-sentence.

He rose, a smile on his lips. Elle was in the hallway, looking ready to bolt. Anne wasn't with her. Perfect.

"Elle," warmth infused his voice, "come on in and meet Gram."

Elle tucked a strand of hair behind her ear. She crept forward and held a hand out to his grandmother.

Her lush lips turned into a genuine smile. "Nice to meet you, uh…"

"Agnes," Gram answered, "but Gram's fine, too. You'd be surprised what I've answered to over the years."

A burst of laughter escaped Elle; she visibly relaxed.

He'd better jump in before Gram became too inquisitive. "Have a seat. Ask Gram anything. She's lived here for four years."

"The first three were in the assisted living unit." Gram settled back in her recliner, happy to have someone new to talk to. "But these old bones are getting too weak to do much on my own. I moved into this room about a year ago."

Elle asked a few more questions pertaining to the units Gram had lived in. Dillon was content to watch, settled in the seat next to Elle.

"Who do you have moving in here?" Gram asked.

Elle smiled faintly, her gaze darting to the window. "My father. He had an accident and needs a place to recover. Once he's well enough, he'll move into an assisted living apartment."

He leaned forward, resting his hand on hers. He didn't know what happened, but his experience with his own father propelled him to comfort her. "I'm sorry, Elle."

Her gaze touched on him before drifting back to Gram. "Thank you, Agnes. I appreciate your openness." She faced Dillon. "I feel much better talking with someone so knowlededgeable. Thank you."

When she stood to leave, he rose with her. Not willing to miss an opportunity. "I'll walk you out. Be right back Gram."

Elle was going to refuse, but Gram interrupted.

"Take your time. We don't play cards on Sundays; I'm not going anywhere."

Elle set a brisk pace down the hallway like she was scared to be seen with him.

"I can find my way out, thanks." Her curt tone didn't dissuade him.

"It's no problem."

Once they were outside, she rounded on him. "Dil—"

She was going to play dirty and let her counselor degree block him from getting to know her, he knew it.

"Elle, it was really nice seeing you outside the office." His charm, rusty as it was, blazed through his smile. "I know you think I came in because my dad was concerned about me," his smile dropped as the subject grew too personal, "but truth is, he was worried about everything in his last days. He left lists for me." He tried to chuckle, but it died off.

"I'm sorry. What'd he pass away from?"

"Pancreatic cancer. Shortly after I got out of the Army, he told me he'd been sick. My uncles decided to sell after that. That way they could enjoy retirement, but be around to help us kids learn to run the farm."

"It was five uncles before five cousins?"

Her curiosity seemed genuine and not clinical. A refreshing change. "One kid from each family. So happens we're all the oldest, too. I'm an only child, but I have other cousins outside of the Walker Five."

"I always wished for a big family." Her expression shuttered and she took a step back like she'd said too much. "I'd better get going."

"Wait." He couldn't let her go. When would they cross

paths again? "I'd really like to talk with you again. Person to person."

Regret filled her features. "I'm sorry, Dillon. It wouldn't be appropriate. And...I really think you should continue seeing someone." She looked around to make sure no one was within earshot. "Have you thought more on AA?"

"Why would I need to?"

"I can't answer that for you."

"Quit being a therapist, Elle. Are you interested in me or not?"

"It wouldn't be appropriate."

"I'm not your patient anymore." He took a deep breath. Showing his frustration would only scare her off and she really was trying to do the right thing in her world. But what if she was the right thing in his world? "Okay, yes, I've thought about AA." After his dad's funeral, he had. "It's too easy to talk myself out of it. What if you go with me? I won't change plans on you."

She recoiled. "Oh God, no."

Whoa. For someone who touted the benefits of the program she seemed horrified at the thought of going herself.

As if sensing how insulting her reaction had been, her eyes widened. "I mean—"

"It wouldn't be appropriate?" He earned her chagrinned expression. "I'm not your client anymore. I'm not a client at all. I'm just asking a friend who knows a little about the subject. Come on. Come with me to break the ice."

"Those meetings are serious, Dillon," she said, her tone chiding.

"I get it."

"I'm sorry."

So was he, but he wasn't giving up on her. "How're you adjusting to Moore?"

The corner of her mouth lifted. "It's different, but I like the slower pace. Less traffic."

"It only gets backed up if there's a combine hogging the highway."

She chuckled. Her tentative smile twisted his gut in knots. "I haven't experienced that yet."

"Where're ya from? No wait. The maroon sweatshirt gave it away."

"Right? I have at least three of these." She paused. Great, she was going to make a break for it— "Your grandma was really nice."

Thank you, Gram. "She's a card. I come see her every Sunday. How's your dad?"

Worry flared in her eyes. "Better. I-I think he'll like it here, at least when he gets to assisted living. It gets lonely for him when I'm at work all day and it's just me and him at night."

Confirmed she was single. "He can't live in senior housing?"

Her sad smile threatened to break his heart. "Perhaps he'd qualify, but he's had cancer, too. Leukemia and combined with the...chronic illness he had before that, he needs assistance."

Had it been just Elle through all that? What had happened to her mom? "Why Moore? Wouldn't a city have more options for him?"

She shook her head, silver glinting off strands of her hair in the sun. "Well, yes, but really expensive. I could make more there, but wouldn't have the flexibility to check on him. Medical bills are still rolling in, so..."

"Their loss, our gain. Don't worry, Gram will get him introduced around. When do you think he'll be released from the hospital?"

"Maybe by next weekend if there's no complications, but

probably the week after. He's young yet, and fairly healthy since chemo forced him to quit— They're optimistic." She tucked a lock of hair behind her ear. Her eyes glistened.

"Are you all right?"

She squeezed her eyes shut and seemed to hold her breath.

He stepped forward, his first instinct to comfort. Would she shove him off, deeply offended?

When she dragged in a shuddering breath, he couldn't just stand by.

"Hey," he said softly and wrapped his arms around her. "Hey. It'll be all right."

She tensed in his embrace, then relaxed into him. Her shoulders shook and a squeak escaped her as she struggled to hold in her cry.

"When he gets settled," he rubbed her back to soothe her, "Gram and I'll give him a proper housewarming."

She abruptly pulled away. "Oh...thanks." Wiping her eyes, she continued putting distance between them. "I need to go."

"Elle." He started for her, but stopped. It'd send her running. "It's okay. It'll be okay."

"I hope so," she mumbled before rushing for her car.

ELLE HELD it together until the grocery store parking lot. She didn't need groceries, she just needed off the road.

After finding a parking spot at the edge of the lot, she parked and slammed her head back on the head rest.

What the hell had she been thinking?

He'd hugged her? She'd broken down in front of him.

"Oh God," she groaned.

What if someone saw? Good-bye job.

Putting her hand to her forehead, she worked through the

worst-case scenario. She'd get fired. Couldn't pay bills. Bankrupt. Move back to the cities and find a good job and put her dad in a cheap-ass home where he'd get shitty care.

Okay. She could survive that.

Likely scenario. No one saw and if they did, only a few knew he was a previous client. Technically, she was no longer involved in his care.

Why had she curled into him for comfort—in public?

Because his touch had felt so good and she'd held in her worries for so long. Out in the open, in the light of day, after a, dare she admit, enjoyable conversation with Agnes, she'd been vulnerable. Because after the cheer and seeing a man bantering back and forth with a clearly loving grandma, she left the nursing home only to have the reality of her dad's situation crash down on her. And she'd been heading home to an empty house to deal with it all.

Rolling her neck, she sat for a few more minutes. Her barren house still waited.

She blew out a breath and threw the car into drive. No amount of waiting would shake the warmth and security of Dillon's arms.

CHAPTER 6

*D*illon swerved to miss a muddy patch on his trip back from town. The weather couldn't decide what it wanted. Freezing rain, followed by sunny but cool days, and rain/snow mix in the forecast.

It'd been two days since the incident with Elle in the parking lot. The urge to call her and see how she was doing rode him hard. But he hadn't dialed her number. Part of him wanted her to let her fingers do the talking.

He'd check with Gram on Sunday. Have her keep an eye out for Elle's dad.

Approaching his house, he spotted Brock's truck parked by the shop.

Brock spoke as soon as Dillon killed the engine and opened the door. "Where the hell have you been? The sun's shining and you're wasting daylight."

Dillon climbed out, but left the case of beer in the cab. No need to repeat Brock's interrogation of the previous week. "Excuse me, Brock, I didn't know I had to call and ask permission to wipe my ass before I take a shit."

Brock stood next to his Ford, glaring at him. "You do

when I'm holding the toilet paper, waiting to use the bathroom. *You* asked me over here to check out the equipment before you worked on the north quarter tomorrow."

"You know where it is, you could've started whenever you wanted." At Brock's stubborn glance at the door, Dillon figured out why his normally mellow cousin was annoyed. "You don't know where your keys are, do you?"

Brock grumbled something unintelligible. Dillon chuckled and was shot a dirty look.

Brock adjusted his hat. "Cash said he called and offered to help get the fields ready before the weather moves in next week."

Dillon's grin faded. "Yeah. Don't need it."

"You haven't needed his help since you two came back home."

"Because I realized how unreliable Cash is." When it counted the most. He worried enough with Cash in charge of the ranching portion of their operation, but at least he'd only cost them money. Dillon didn't want to see a cow or horse get hurt, but it wouldn't keep him up at night like—

"I'll let you into the shop," Dillon grumbled. When he reached the door, he stopped and swore.

Brock craned his neck around him. "No fucking way! They broke in?"

Dillon nudged the open door with its dented metal and gouged wood. The lights were off and a chemical tang hung in the air.

Both he and Brock sniffed. Brock guessed the smell first. "Paint?"

Dillon flicked the lights on. Words flew out of their mouths that their mamas would've used a bar of Ivory soap on not too long ago.

"Call the police." Brock whipped out his phone and Dillon entered to determine the rest of the damage.

The two main tractors stored in his shop had been vandalized. The yellow spray paint was the most obvious, but when Dillon got closer, he saw the tires on the smaller tractor were trashed, opened up with black, gaping holes. The fucker probably had had to use a machete to cut into them. Or a carving knife and a lot of rage.

He texted Aaron and Travis to check their shops and equipment. Aaron's shop held the combines for harvest and Travis stored all the haying equipment. They both lived farther from town than Dillon, so maybe he was the only one targeted—easier access?

Dillon assessed the damage while waiting for the deputy to arrive to take pictures and ask a truckload of questions. Except for the tires, it was all nuisance repair. Yellow squiggles covered both tractors, garish against the original red paint. To keep from smashing anything breakable, Dillon tried to look on the bright side. At least no swear words were scrawled in the obnoxiously-colored paint. And those two pieces of equipment were mostly used on the main stretch of road that he and all his cousins lived on. It'd save a little face. Someone might notice the new detailing on the tractors out in the fields and wonder if it was a new farm logo.

The crunch of tires on his driveway signaled the deputy had arrived. He went back out to meet him. Max Steelman, one of the county's finest and an old family friend, greeted him.

"Another vandalism?" Max asked.

"A little more obvious this time." Dillon's phone started ringing. Aaron. He waved at Max to go on in. "Brock's in there and can show you, but it'll be clear right away what kind of damage was done."

Max retrieved his camera from the patrol car. Dillon answered the call to pass on the bad news.

He rubbed his temples. And here he'd thought the phone

call from Cash cast a dark cloud over his day.

Shoulda picked up two cases of beer.

"I TOLD ya we'd have a house warming."

Elle froze at the baritone. Her dad glanced at the doorway in surprise, then at her.

She plastered a friendly smile on her face and waved Dillon in. Introducing him to her dad, she skipped how she knew him. Her dad would have enough tact to ask when they were alone, giving Elle time to think of an answer that wasn't the truth.

"Dillon, this my dad, Gary Brady."

They shook hands. Her dad looked so diminutive with his blanket-wrapped form prone in the bed and a farm boy towering over him. Gary had never been as tall or broad as Dillon in the first place and then alcohol and leukemia had eaten the muscle right off him.

Dillon shoved his hands in his pockets and studied the room. "I see you got settled."

If by settled, he meant a few pairs of her dad's sweats and a rocker glider for her to hang out in, then…yeah.

"I'm going to bring a little bit each time I visit." The touch of defensiveness in her tone wasn't on purpose, but the more she was around Dillon without the buffer of her office environment, the more he scrambled her senses.

It'd help if his clothing was rumpled and his eyes were bloodshot, but since it was four in the afternoon, he might be past the hangover stage. Instead, an apparently healthy, virile man choked out all the air in dad's room, leaving her short of breath, butterflies spasming in her belly.

"Lemme know if you need help. I've got four other guys at my beck and call with strong backs."

"Thanks for the offer. I'm sure I'll be fine." Rejecting help was a reflex for her. Only this time, there was no staggering dad at home to hide.

"Thanks for offering, Dillon." Her dad shifted and winced. "That's great knowing Elle has assistance if needed. So, what do you do for work?"

Dillon chose a seat next to her on the metal chair the nursing home supplied. His heat and fresh scent radiated off him until she was pressed to the farthest side of the rocker.

Why was she so aware of him?

"I farm north of town, the Walker Five. We have both a farming and ranching operation, but I stick with the farm unless it's time to move and work cattle."

Her dad chuckled. "It's a whole different world out here." He sighed. "I'm glad for the slower pace."

"We don't get too worked up in Moore unless the street dance gets rained out."

The guys went back and forth, discussing the crazy not-quite spring weather for this time of year.

Elle studied her fingernails. Chitchat wasn't part of her personal life. She'd never thought she'd missed it, because her days were filled with talking and listening. But this threatened to be nice, to be enjoyable.

"Listen." Dillon sat forward to address them both. "Gram is ready to give the grand tour, get you into all the cliques. You like pinochle, she's got a partner for you. Want to be on the bird feeding rotations, she knows the scheduler personally. Say the word."

"I appreciate it." Her dad's eyes lit with excitement, but with an undercurrent of anxiety from the anticipation of dealing with people. Those old feelings that drove him deep into the bottle in the first place.

"But hey, if you want to be left the hell alone, Gram will fend 'em all off." Dillon's grin caused her to grin, too.

Her dad laughed. "Some days, right?"

She peeked at her watch, and Dillon caught her action.

"Can I walk you out again, Elle?"

Before she could decline, her dad interjected. "Go on. I've got the DVD player and those new movies you brought, peanut. Go home and get some rest. You've got a full week ahead of you and they'll be bringing dinner soon."

Make a scene or roll with it?

She collected her purse and gave her dad a kiss.

"Nice to meet you, Gary." Dillon followed her out. "I've been wondering how you're doing."

He...worried about her? "I'm fine."

They meandered through the hallways, just two people with loved ones in the home. A nice excuse for her to be around him.

Stepping outside, she mourned the fading sun. The crisp air promised snow, but the weather forecaster wasn't sure exactly when. Just sometime this week.

"Take out your phone. I want you to call me."

She swung to stare at him. "What?"

"You don't know anyone and if you get into a bind, I want you to have someone to call."

Her hand twitched to do as he asked, but she curled her fingers around her tote strap.

"Elle." He rolled his eyes toward her, his mouth lifted in a teasing smile. "If it storms and you're stuck in a drift you can't shovel out, who are you going to call?"

"I'm sure there's a tow truck I can call."

He nodded. "There is, but what if it's after ten at night and you're going home from here? Ten-Four Towing shuts down after six. Vicki put her foot down and said no more emergency calls."

Her brow furrowed as she tried to come up with a plan. "I'll call the police."

"Yep. They can take you home. Can't dig you out until Ten-Four opens again at eight a.m."

Scowling at him, she dug her phone out and handed it to him. A thrill shot through her and she stomped it back into place. He punched in his digits and his phone rang.

He silenced his and turned her phone back over. "You need anything, you call."

She tucked her phone back into place but felt the weight of his stare.

"Okay?" he stressed.

She couldn't help but smile, hated to admit how nice it was to have someone looking out for her. "Got it." Reluctant to walk away, she took a side step, but he stepped with her.

"You haven't eaten supper yet?"

Her stomach chose that moment to rumble and she pressed in on her belly. "No. I have leftovers waiting for me at home."

"Let's go grab a bite."

She stifled an automatic no. He'd been so nice and considerate. "I…"

Her automatic response of *It wouldn't be appropriate* stalled. If only she was going somewhere more emotionally comforting than her empty house, surrounded by her dad's stuff, and bills piled on the counter…

"I'll drive." He nodded toward a flashy pickup.

As he swaggered toward it, she glanced between the vehicle and him. Her car could probably fit into the box of the black pickup. For the first time, she allowed herself to admire the breadth of his shoulders and how his long-sleeved shirt tucked into a narrow waist. She stopped before she reached his butt. No need to torture a girl.

She opened her mouth to let him know she couldn't go, but no words formed.

He reached the passenger side and opened the door,

waiting for her.

Without permission from her reasonable brain, her feet shuffled toward him.

The grin that lit his face was worth it, yet guilt began to build. She shouldn't be doing this, shouldn't be getting his hopes up. They could talk over food.

"What's open?" The pickup was so tall, she had to use the running board to climb inside.

He stood with one hand on the door, the other against the frame. A casual position, but his body draped next to her like that shorted her thinking.

"There's the diner along the highway. They have a ton of choices."

Now was her chance to make her apologies, she couldn't go. Gently nudge him out of the way and slide down.

"Sounds good."

His blue eyes twinkled as he shut the door. She stared straight ahead.

What was she doing?

The enormous cab of the truck shrank to a quarter of its size when he got in.

Once they were on the way, he draped a hand over the steering wheel and glanced at her. "How's your dad really doing?"

Genuine concern was in his voice and she appreciated it. Betsy and a couple of her other coworkers had also been checking in. How different it was when Elle could actually discuss her father's health. When he'd been deep into his alcoholism, Elle had isolated her and her dad so badly that no one knew what went on at home.

"He's good. I don't think he's crazy about the nursing home portion; he's one of the youngest in there. But his assisted living apartment will be ready soon and he's recovering quickly so I'm sure he'll move in within weeks."

"Good to hear. How'd it happen?"

She told him the story of coming home to find her dad at the bottom of the stairs.

"Good thing he has you."

"Yeah." Story of her life. He would've been dead from malnutrition a decade ago.

"Here it is." He pulled into a small restaurant she'd passed several times but had never tried.

She swallowed hard and fiddled with her purse. What if she knew someone in there? What if one of her coworkers decided to eat out tonight? She should've gone home instead.

To her great relief, she recognized no one.

Dinner was a revelation. She peppered Dillon with questions about the nursing home. He answered, entertaining her with Gram's stories of life in the home. Elle could watch him tell stories for hours. His voice, his expressions, so alive, lacking all the panicked melancholy she'd felt for years.

"Gram used to bring a cowbell to my football games."

Elle tried not to laugh with a mouthful of food. Gram raising a ruckus in the stands sounded like the kind of grandma Elle would've loved.

"What's your favorite team?" Dillon asked.

A warm glow ignited within her at his sweet smile. "The team that's finished playing."

"Oh, so it's like that." He chuckled.

"It is. I like football movies, though."

"It's a start." His eyes twinkled and her warm glow grew hotter. How was it possible he was growing better looking?

Afraid, he'd start asking her questions, she asked him to list his favorite football movies, what number he'd been, anything she could think of. Her anxiety that they'd run into someone she knew had diminished, but she still hadn't relaxed fully. She wanted to, she realized with a start as she watched him polish off his meal. Her craving to be at ease around this man had grown exponentially during their time together.

"What about you?" he asked.

And there it was. She set her fork down, glad she'd finished her roast because her stomach had soured. *Be yourself.* "There's not much."

He gave her the *really?* look.

Her mouth quirked. "All right. I was born and raised in Minneapolis. My mom left us before I was teenager and it was me and my dad. I went to the University of Minnesota. That about sums it up."

"Ever married?"

"God, no."

He laughed. "Whoa. Touchy subject?"

Her cheeks warmed. "No, but my life hasn't been marriage friendly. There was school, more school, work to pay for school, and then Dad developed leukemia. Now it's work to pay for his care."

"What'd he do for a living?"

Ah, yes. One of the two questions she hated the most. The other one involved anything with her mother because Elle didn't know. No clue where her mom lived, worked, or if she'd married the man she'd run off with.

As for the subject of her dad's employment... It used to depend on the day.

"A little bit of everything." Her answer used to be *He's in between jobs,* which was usually true. "But getting sick forced him into early retirement." Not that he'd saved up anything for real retirement. All of those funds had been consumed in liquid form.

"You're the sole bread winner. Wow." He nodded and smiled at a couple their age that walked by. They glanced curiously between her and Dillon before moving on.

She dug in her purse for her debit card. "I'd better get home."

"My treat." He tossed some bills on the table.

Staring at the bills, she fought the swell of panic that this seemed too close to a date. Shit, she didn't have any cash to pay him back. "I'll just grab some money from the ATM."

His hand landed on hers until she stopped. "It's okay, Elle. I got it."

"Thanks." Hastily, she stood and marched outside to his vehicle. Dillon was quiet behind her, but he opened the pickup door for her.

"If I'd have known I'd be entertaining a pretty lady today, I would've washed my truck."

She couldn't help but smile at his compliment. His black pickup still held a healthy shine under the fine sheen of dust it sported.

He hopped in and fired up the engine.

Elle snapped her seatbelt but Dillon didn't move. Elle peered around to see what he was waiting on. A family was loading into the car on his left, their small children chittering excitedly and gripping colorful balloons the restaurant handed out.

A balloon popped. One of the kids let out a wail and started to cry.

Dillon jerked, his knuckles white around the steering wheel. He glared at the car, but his gaze swept their surroundings in a way she'd only seen on TV, on soldier or cop shows.

"Are you all right?" she asked, softly.

Visibly relaxing, he smiled at her, but it didn't hold the same authenticity as before. "Of course."

The drive back was quiet.

She struggled to think up a question that didn't sound like she was at work. "What'd you do for school?"

His eyebrows rose in surprise. Must be because she made a move to get to know him. "It took forever, but I finally got a degree in business while I was in the Army."

"Online?"

"Sucked, but it's done."

"That takes dedication."

He snorted. "Especially when my cousin wanted to go hit the bars every night. No wonder Cash never finished his degree."

"Cash is the cousin you deployed with?"

"Yes, and he never had to be responsible because I always was. We managed to get stationed together for four years. It was a little too much closeness. Here we are."

He parked next to her car in the empty nursing home lot.

With her hand on the door handle, she turned to face him. "Thank you for dinner."

He leaned in to close the distance. "Anytime." His eyes landed on her lips.

Her better judgment didn't stand a chance as his mouth captured hers.

He tasted hot, spicy, like the habanero ranch he'd had with his fries. His lips were firm, the hint of stubble from his chin only increasing the sensation.

Her hands left their purchase to clutch at his jacket. He palmed the back of her neck, pulling her closer, coaxing open her mouth. She opened greedily for him. All of her pent up, forbidden emotions regarding Dillon roared in her brain, clambering to get closer to him.

The first swipe of his tongue against hers released a moan. He. Felt. So. Good. She slid her hands up his broad shoulders, loving the feel of muscle so hard, so defined. When her hands reached the bare skin of his neck she splayed her fingers over his hair, trying to touch as much of him as possible.

Their tongues tangled, danced, caressed. If the damn console weren't in the way, she'd be pressed to him from head to toe.

With the advantage of his height, he leaned farther over, his free hand landing on her thigh. It felt like a branding, staking his claim on her body. He devoured her and she gave herself to him, lost in the pleasure of his caress on her leg. He managed to work his way under her jacket, under her sweatshirt.

She gasped into his mouth when his rough, calloused hand stroked her side.

More. She wanted more.

Arching her back, she wanted to feel his touch all over. She was wearing too damn many clothes.

Massaging his way up her torso, she whimpered softly when he closed in on her sensitive nipples.

Yes. Please, yes.

She hoped he read minds because she couldn't pry her mouth away from his for anything.

His thumb brushed her beaded nipple through her cotton bra. It wasn't enough for her; it wasn't enough for him. Soon, her entire breast was cupped by his palm.

It wasn't enough!

She was unzipping her jacket when a horn wailed down the road.

Elle pulled back sharply with a gasp, whipping her head toward the sound.

Oh God, did someone see them?

Two cars faded into the distance. They must've been honking at each other.

Horror dawned; her eyes widened.

Dillon was breathing heavy, his look fierce with desire. He'd calmed slightly, gauging her reaction. His lips were wet from their kissing, his hand had gone back down to her leg.

He wasn't just a former client. He was *that* man she swore she'd never get involved with. Because no matter how sweet and caring he was, if he had a drinking problem, she couldn't involve her heart.

"I can't— That was wrong. I've got to go."

"Elle, wait."

She grabbed her purse and hopped out of the pickup.

He waited for her at the box of the pickup by the time she made it around.

"Elle."

She stepped around him. "No. I'm sorry. I was way out of line."

"We did nothing wrong."

"I'm sorry, Dillon." He followed her all the way to her car door.

Thank heaven for car remotes, because fumbling with a key would be icing on her humiliation cake.

She sat down in the driver's seat, but she couldn't shut the door. Dillon held it open.

"Can we talk?"

"There's nothing to talk about. That can never happen again."

"I'm still going to call and make sure you're doing okay."

Oh crap, he had her number. She was going to tell him not to, but like before, she couldn't bring herself to say no. She only gave him a sad smile.

He shut the door and stepped back, a grim expression lined his face.

She drove away. He watched her, his tall form fading in the taillights.

His kiss lingered on her lips, her breast ached to be touched by him again.

Stop. Just *stop*. He was off limits, and that's the way it had to stay.

CHAPTER 7

Sunday night had been hell. Monday morning had been a headache-filled form of torture. Even Dillon admitted to himself he'd had a few too many drinks after the way the night ended with Elle.

By Monday afternoon, after hours in the field, he'd decided it hadn't been a failure. He had pushed her past her boundaries with him, but maybe she'd see there was so much potential between them. He couldn't be the only one to feel the high level of attraction between them.

Tuesday morning and he was fresh as a daisy, having fallen into an exhausted sleep the night before.

His feeling was figurative only. The rains in the dark hours of morning had made for an interesting adventure when Brock had called him. Cash needed help getting a calf out of a mud pit. Poor thing had fallen and gotten trampled by the other cows, too weak to get out of the muck.

Back at his place, he couldn't enter the house until he cleaned himself up. Muddy boots were the first to go before he stripped entirely—a huge benefit to living rurally. He dumped his dirty laundry in the washer.

There'd be mud chunks in the wash for at least three loads.

Showered and in fresh clothes, he watched the clock. Elle got done with work at five, give or take a few minutes. He'd call her at a quarter after.

Tapping his fingers against the counter, he stared out the kitchen window at his shop. The vandalized tractor was inside. Brock had rattle-canned over the worst of it, finding the closest red to match. The paint job was garish, but better than yellow scribbles all over.

The shop was kept locked twenty-four/seven. If the asshole who was messing with them broke in, at least there was a chance he'd leave evidence.

Dillon checked his phone. Time to call. He could wait until the weekend, but he didn't want her thinking he'd moved on.

It rang. And rang.

Maybe she wasn't out of work yet.

Rang some more.

Maybe *she'd* moved on.

"Hello." Her tone wasn't that of the thrilled girl who'd finally gotten called by the man of her dreams.

"Hey, Elle." Words left him, his breath hitched. Good grief, he hadn't batted an eye when he'd asked a girl out for the first time before. "I was…checking in on you."

"I'm doing fine." She spoke cautiously.

"Good. How 'bout I take you out for dinner? Or I could bring something over."

She didn't respond immediately. "Dillon, I can't see you."

"Because it wouldn't be appropriate." His tone was flat.

"Yes. What happened," her voice dropped low, "Sunday night can't happen again."

"I'm not your client anymore."

"But you were."

"And what, that's it? We're done. Not a chance?"

"It's not just that—" When she cut off, he waited for the reason, but nothing. "I can't see you anymore, Dillon. Not on a personal or professional level. I'm sorry, good-bye."

He stared at his phone after she disconnected. That was it? Done.

He tossed it on the counter and slapped his hands on the countertop. Glaring out the window, he cursed himself for the hundredth time for making that damn appointment, for letting his family's insinuations get to him.

And all the questions. *What's with you and Cash? What happened over there? Did you kill anyone?*

They all watched too much TV.

He'd let his guilt over leaving home as fast as he could and coming home to find out his dad was dying persuade him to seek counseling.

He slammed his fists down. There was nothing *wrong* with him. The shit between him and Cash was Cash's issue. If his cousin could live with what his irresponsibility cost him, so be it.

But the shadow had been cast on him, too, and it'd cost him Elle. The only woman in a long time who'd been more than a few hours of fun.

The last thing he wanted to do was close himself in the shop alone and angry at himself and his dad. Then he'd feel like utter shit because he was angry at a dead man.

The clouds chose that moment to dump more rain because the weather couldn't decide what to do this time of year. He couldn't drag out the tractor and get into the fields.

His phone pinged with a text from Brock.

Rain day, bitch. The Place.

The Place was actually Barley 'n' Hops, but it's "the place" they always went. Staring at the invite, he realized he hadn't eaten lunch yet.

He punched in his reply. *Beat you there, bro.*

CHAPTER 8

*E*lle adjusted the box as she walked into her dad's room. "I brought more of your stuff from home, some more clothes."

Her dad offered a smile. "Great, Elle, but I'm more glad to see you."

She set about unpacking and filling his dresser and tiny closet. Tonight, she was actually grateful to hang out with her dad. After the phone call from Dillon, her house had seemed an echoing cavern.

Dillon.

She sighed and concentrated on putting socks away. Her head knew she made the right decision, but her heart screamed and rallied against it. If he hadn't walked into her office, she would've been jumping up and down at her good fortune.

Aside from his hard-working background and business ownership, he was so *good-looking*. His teasing eyes had filled with concern—for her. How strong he felt when he wrapped his arms around her. How safe she'd felt.

Her dad grumbled behind her. "It's raining out. You don't have to sit here with an old man and drive home in it."

"It might clear up."

"If it wasn't for that damn chemo, my bones wouldn't be so brittle. I wouldn't be here where you'd have to be out in the elements."

If wasn't for your damn drinking, you might not have developed leukemia and needed chemo.

He started on his normal rant when he found himself in an embarrassing situation. His daughter caring for him like he was ninety instead of sixty had him blaming the world, everyone but himself. As always.

She'd give him this time and stay quiet. As always.

A nursing home was a hard transition for anyone, and he was younger than 95 percent of the residents.

Shoving his shirts into the drawer, she uttered noncommittal answers. It was this or go home. She'd stay long enough to watch the ten o'clock news before heading out.

Dillon glared at Cash while he flirted and played pool with a couple of girls they'd gone to school with. One was married but she didn't act like it—not around his cousin. The other girl pressed up against Cash every chance she got.

"Can I grab you another?" said the perky server beside Dillon.

He'd met her before, the few times he'd been here during the winter. She always let him know she had no plans after closing time. He'd never taken her up on it; if things turned south between them, he didn't want to have to quit coming to The Place.

"I'll take another," he told her.

Laughter caught his attention, bringing his incensed gaze back to his cousin.

She glanced at the pool table and misinterpreted his irritation as being toward Cash getting all the attention. "I don't have any plans once my shift is done."

"I'll keep that in mind." His kept his words pleasant, but uninterested.

"Stick around. You won't regret it," she purred.

Dillon stared at her ass swaying across the bar, not moved in the slightest. Regret. He had plenty of it and doubted the server would be as regret-free as she claimed. All the room in his mind was being taken up by his asshole, irresponsible cousin and a pretty little counselor who'd ditched him.

He finished his beer and his server delivered another with a flirty smile.

Taking a long swig, he relished the feeling of the first pull, when the beer was still ice cold with all its kick. He joked he drank so fast because he hated flat, warm beer.

"Hey, Dill," Cash called, his arm draped around the single chick as they walked toward the door. "I'm taking off."

Dillon held his arms out like, *what the fuck?* Brock had taken off early. Travis had left with his girlfriend and Aaron had stayed home. Probably counting seeds. He got all wound up around planting season.

Cash shrugged and continued out the door.

Irresponsible prick.

He pulled out his phone to call Aaron to drive his ass to town to pick him up. The phone clattered to the table. Slippery little bugger. Some of the numbers were fuzzy. Naw. It wasn't the phone. It was him. Finally, he dialed Aaron.

It rang and rang.

Phone calls weren't his thing today. Looked like he was sleeping one off in his truck.

Not the first time.

Making a motion for anther beer, he figured he might as well have another if he wasn't going anywhere.

ELLE PEERED THROUGH HER WIPERS. Rain came down hard and she was angry with herself. She'd fallen asleep watching the news and her dad thought he was doing her a favor letting her sleep.

She would've missed the nasty weather if she'd left on time. Now it was after one in the morning and she still had her work clothes and lunch to ready for work, then try to grab a few more hours so she wasn't a mess tomorrow.

Sitting forward, she peered out the car window. At least the rain would help wash the dirt and sand off the roads leftover from winter. The steady rain they'd gotten all day certainly helped, but this downpour would flush everything clean.

A familiar pickup caught her eye. It was sitting in the otherwise empty parking lot of Barley 'n' Hops.

Jealously flared when the question of who Dillon went home with ran through her mind. No matter. He wasn't her business, literally or figuratively, and she'd expressly told him so. And he'd apparently listened and found someone else immediately. At a bar.

Still, it stung being reminded how forgettable she was.

She spared one last look as she drove past. Startled, she slowed down.

A streetlight highlighted a form slumped in the passenger seat. She pulled into the lot and parked next to the pickup. To make sure he was all right, she told herself.

Wishing she kept an umbrella in her car, she climbed out and went to the window his head leaned against. She rapped on it.

He didn't move.

She knocked harder. Her hair was saturated with rain, streams ran down her face, and she wondered why the hell she was going through the effort.

To make sure he was okay, she reminded herself.

He shifted, but remained sleeping. Or passed out.

She was getting downright soggy through and through. Picking the point next to his ear, she tapped hard against the glass.

He jerked his head up and squinted out the window. His arm shifted like he reached for a sidearm he wasn't wearing. A very telling reaction.

She moved out of the way when he opened the door.

"Elle?" Alcohol permeated the cab and his breath.

"I stopped to see if you were all right."

Bleary eyed, he scanned the downpour and empty streets. "Just sleeping one off cuz Cash left me hanging."

"It's raining." Would the nice and dry farm boy take the hint?

He gave her a lazy smile, still extremely good-looking in a sloppy, intoxicated way. "It's not in my truck if you want to hop in."

She ignored the invitation. "Do you need me to drive you home, Dillon?"

He craned his neck to look around her. "That little puddle jumper would get eaten alive on the roads out to my place." His eyes swept her body and unwelcome heat smoldered in unwanted places. "You're getting wet, Elle."

She cut off the direction he tried taking the conversation. "I'd better get home. Take care of yourself, Dillon."

He slumped back in his chair. So unfair how good he looked in jeans and a button-up with dressier cowboy boots than he normally wore. But that way lay heartbreak.

"'Night, Elle." He popped his head up. "Thanks for stopping to check on me."

The sincerity in his voice stopped her from leaving. Not just sincerity, but…sadness? Like her leaving him in the rain was expected behavior. "Come on, Dillon. You can sleep it off on my couch."

Those blue eyes lit with surprise. "It'd probably be warmer, huh?"

She nodded and stepped back when he climbed out. He swung the door shut and swayed on his feet. If he went down, he'd take both of them because there was no way she could catch him.

He folded his body into her car while she went around to her side.

Dillon stayed quiet for a few blocks. It was hard for him to hold his head up, but she refrained from asking him how much he'd had to drink. Answer: more than enough.

He wiped rain drops off his face. "I should've stayed home. I hate going to the bar. Too many people, too many questions."

Too many questions? "Why were you out tonight?"

"Rain day. Originally, I was hoping to take a pretty lady out for dinner, but she blew me off."

She stayed quiet and hoped he'd keep going so she didn't have to explain herself any further.

"The guys wanted to go out and I hadn't eaten yet." He gave a disgusted snort. "Then Cash left me for a piece of —I figured I might as well stay indoors before I had to catch some shut eye in my truck."

"It's not my fault, or Cash's, that you drank too much."

He swung his gaze toward her. "Didn't say that. I'm allowed to go out and have fun."

She pulled into her driveway and waited for the garage door to open. Now wasn't the time to insist that yeah, he did.

He'd likely not remember any of it, and it wasn't her battle, not this time. Elle wasn't in the mood for dude repair. It didn't work on her dad, and she sure as hell wouldn't do it for a personal relationship.

After the garage door shut them in, it dawned on her that she had Dillon Walker in her home. Probably not the best decision she could've made, but leaving him in his truck in the storm would've kept her up all night.

"I'll show you where the couch is and get you some blankets."

"Elle…"

He sounded like he was going to make more excuses, beg her forgiveness, whatever. She'd heard it all before from her dad. "Dillon, I'm soaked, cold, and tired. I have to get up in a few hours for work. Let's just get inside."

He stared at her with glassy eyes before he nodded and got out, waiting for her to unlock the door into her house.

Dumping her stuff on the counter, she slid off her shoes and coat. He did the same, his movements jerky, unrefined, not how she was used to seeing him. Her tall, swaggering farm boy wasn't this man she brought home.

"You can have my dad's room. The bed will fit you better than the couch."

He had one hip propped against the counter, shoulders drooped, assessing her. It was her hold-everything-counter since it was right next to the door from the garage and too far away from anything in the kitchen to be useful.

Instead of waiting for him to say something and getting dragged into another conversation best left to a different counselor, she spoke first. "The door's open; it's the first room on the left. You can let yourself out tomorrow when you wake up, just flip the lock on the door knob when you go. Don't worry about the deadbolt." No clue how he'd get back to his truck, but again, not her issue.

He kicked off the counter and used a hand on the wall to steady himself. "Why do I feel like my parents just busted me and my cousins for having a bonfire in the south pasture while they were out of town?"

She was tired, chilled to the bone from rescuing him, so her speech lost its filter. "Why do I feel like I traded one drunk for another?" Confusion drew his brows low, but she'd had enough. "Good night, Dillon."

Storming to her room, she shut the door and leaned against it. Within a minute, she heard his soft footsteps enter her dad's room.

Why had he made his appointment with *her*? Why did he have to be so damn sexy? She couldn't let one handsome war vet farmer derail her plans, couldn't waste her career getting involved with him.

Not when her mother's absence showed her exactly how that would end.

illon groaned and rolled over. He was stiff, but his headache wasn't terrible. He pried his eyelids open and didn't recognize the room he was in. The events of the previous night—and really early morning—rolled through his mind.

Cash leaving. After a couple more beers, he'd checked into his pickup to sleep it off, keeping to the passenger seat. Any cops stopping by wouldn't nail him with a DUI thinking he'd passed out in the driver's seat before he could leave.

He'd learned a few tricks in the Army.

Glancing at the clock, he squeezed his eyes shut and wished the world would stop time.

Nine o'clock. Two hours after he'd normally be out and working. His phone vibrated with a text.

All he'd brought with him were the clothes on his back and the phone in his pocket. Digging it out, he swore and dropped it back on the bed.

Where r u?

He was supposed to meet Brock to check out a new tractor, and not just because of the vandalism on the old one.

They'd limped it along long enough, poured more and more money into it. It was time to upgrade with the new style using tracks instead of tires, and newer technology. Hell, any technology.

A tractor with tracks. Track vehicles rolling around the farm like he was back in the Army.

He blew out a breath. Dillon needed to face the day and Brock needed a call back.

"Dude," his cousin answered.

"I know, sorry. Are you headed to town yet?"

"Five minutes before I'm at the implement dealership."

"Can you swing by and pick me up?" Dillon hung his head down, waiting for the barrage of questions. He should've known with Brock it'd be minimal.

"Where?"

Good question. Dillon had only paid attention to the beautiful driver and not where she'd taken him.

"Hold on."

"You don't where you're at?" Brock sounded one part amused and two parts shocked.

"It's not what you think."

"Riiight."

Dillon kept the phone to his ear as he walked through the empty house and into the kitchen. Maybe there'd be some mail or something on the counter so he wouldn't have to go outside to track down the house number and street name.

"Elle Brady found me sleeping in my pickup and brought me to her place."

"Who's she?"

A frustrating woman. "I started seeing her when I tried some counseling. Then she fired me because I'm a man and she's a gorgeous woman and I liked her."

Silence.

"She let me have her dad's old room." Like he had to justify it, or her and the appropriateness of it all.

He found a pile of mail on the counter. The top envelope looked like a medical bill and was addressed to Elle's dad, Gary Brady.

Dillon rattled off the address to Brock and disconnected. He studied his surroundings and his gaze landed back on the pile. Were all of those bills? He had a lot, but they ran a big operation and all the bills came to him and he passed them onto Aaron for accounting. Shuffling the stack, he replaced them as he found them. With the place to himself after Elle's generosity, snooping didn't feel right.

Brock would arrive soon. Dillon double checked his clothing. They were good enough to go tractor shopping, but he should clean up. He went searching for the bathroom.

The image that greeted him in the mirror didn't look half bad. His hair needed a good finger-combing and his eyes were only slightly bloodshot. He used some of Elle's mouth-wash and went back to the kitchen.

A pen and notepad sat by the stack of mail, so he scrawled a quick note to Elle. Would she call him like he asked? He'd guess no. He'd been acting responsible last night, but he suspected she thought otherwise.

Dillon headed to the front door to go out and wait for Brock. The only artwork on the walls were professional paintings that matched the décor. No pictures of family, no pictures of people. Nothing from the earth-toned walls or the decorative window treatments suggested her dad cared for the place. Elle's touch should be all over the place, but instead her dwelling was… bland.

He recalled her office. Same vibe—very few personal touches and no pictures.

In comparison, his own place appeared wild and crazy. His family was huge and since he'd bought his house from his parents, they'd left a lot of the pictures behind. Pictures of him from 4H wins to graduation dominated the walls. The hallways on both levels were lined with family photos of aunts, uncles, and cousins.

He really didn't know much about her, but he had a sneaking suspicion that her life hadn't been as rich and boisterous as his. Her barren walls and sparse living area were a direct reflection of how she lived life.

He could show her a good time.

A honk jolted him out of his pondering. He went out to meet Brock, locking the door behind him.

The giant F350 rumbled on the quiet street. For Elle's sake, Dillon hoped none of her neighbors were home. He didn't want to damage her reputation. If people wanted to gossip about her and Dillon, he wanted to make damn sure they had a reason to.

After being rescued by her, and seeing the stark interior of her house, getting through Elle Brady's shell was going to be harder than he thought.

Dillon settled into the passenger seat before Brock spoke. "We need to go to your place to see if everything's okay when we're done in town." Brock glanced over at him, frowning. "I found tracks around the door to my shop. They aren't mine and nobody else has been out there."

HAD HE LEFT YET?

Forcing herself to focus on her two o'clock client, she succeeded in taking her mind off the sleeping man she'd left in her home.

When she woke for work, she'd tiptoed around the house. The thought of having him alert and moving around her home while she was in it was too much for her to bear. But...

since he hadn't closed the bedroom door all the way, she'd checked on him. Made sure he was all right—the excuse that always worked.

"Elle?"

Her client had asked a question and she'd totally missed it. Because she was thinking about Dillon.

"I'm sorry, can you repeat that?"

With superhuman effort she made it through her appointments and even managed to help her clients. She yawned and stared at her paperwork. Dillon aside, it'd been a late night.

Finally, the workday ended. Betsy popped her head in, looking ready to slip right back out the door. "It's the second Wednesday of the month. Remember—Mental Health Wednesday? Gonna meet us for a drink?"

Elle paused putting her jacket on. Normally, she declined because she had her dad waiting for her at home. Her empty house would only remind her of the handsome farm boy and who'd been in there just this morning.

"Sure. Where we going?"

Betsy's face lit with a surprised grin. Elle turned down every Mental Health Wednesday invite in her time here, but dear Betsy continued to invite Elle to each social event the clinic put on. And they put on a lot, not just their excuse-to-go-out-every-month Wednesday.

"We go to The Funky Corral. I'll save you a spot at the table. We don't usually stay long, but they're forecasting snow, so we'll leave a bit earlier than usual."

Her friend rushed off. Elle smiled to herself and finished gathering her purse and lunch bag.

She had friends! Sort of. She was closest to Betsy, but maybe now she could move beyond superficial friendliness with the others. If she was going to make Moore her home, it'd be nice to actually socialize once in a while.

She quickly phoned her dad to check on him. Some habits died hard, and her persistent guilt didn't help. An emotion that had no place when her dad seemed to be thriving. He was growing more excited about transitioning to assisted living, talking animatedly about game nights, movie showings, the library, and the various activity groups—all thanks to Agnes Walker.

She sighed. Both Elle and her dad had needed a change in routine.

Humming happily to herself, Elle locked up her office and tried not to dance to her car.

The hum stopped when she saw a guy hanging out by her vehicle in the nearly empty lot. Empty, but for the giant type of pickup all too common in Moore. She grabbed her key card for the building back out of her purse, intending to turn and flee inside and…what?

Call the cops and say there's a dude standing in a public place? Wait until he left? Good enough.

The panicked look must've registered on her face, because the guy spoke. "Elle Brady?"

"Yeah," she said slowly, suspicion heavy in the one word.

She didn't recognize him, would've remembered if she met him before. It was like hot farm boys grew on trees around here. He was tall with a solid build and wore a black hat that'd seen cleaner days with coal black hair sticking out from underneath. The way he stood, between his monster of a vehicle and her dwarfed car, reminded her of Dillon.

"I'm Brock Walker, Dillon's cousin."

That explained it. So far Betsy was right about the Walker Five. How devastating were the other three cousins?

He shoved his hands in his jean pockets, as if he was chewing on what to say next.

"Hi." It sounded more like a question when the word left her mouth. Then it occurred to her there must be a reason why he was here. "Is Dillon all right?" She inched closer as adrenaline spilled into her veins at the thought of Dillon being hurt.

"Yes." He rushed on when he saw her face. "No, not like that. I picked him up from your place. When we went back to his truck, it was missing."

"Stolen?"

Brock nodded. "The fucker—sorry—whoever took it crashed it into the campground. The place is still closed for the season, but several of their lots were torn up, ruined. The main office was where they found the truck parked —inside it."

Elle's eyes widened. Someone intentionally rammed it into a building? "Was anyone hurt?"

"No, the whole place is shut down until May; no one was there." Brock took a deep breath and leveled her with a serious look. "Dillon can't prove he wasn't driving. He won't tell them where he was last night, and all the cops received was a report that he had been seen drinking too much and squealing away from the bar."

From Brock's bleak look, she concluded why he was there. "He won't tell them because he's worried about getting me into trouble at work. And you want me to head to the station and let them know he was with me all night."

"I don't want you to get in trouble, Elle, but something like this could tank our operation. The campground owner is pissed and threatening all kinds of legal action."

The fire of adrenaline faded away, her shoulders sagged. Dillon trying to protect her could cost five families their legacy. "I need to make a call first and then I'll go to the police department."

Brock didn't crack a smile. "I appreciate it. I'm sorry you got dragged into this mess. First our tractors and equipment are getting tampered with, and now the damage is escalating."

"You guys have been having issues like this for a while?"

He nodded. "No clue why, but it's getting expensive, and dangerous."

The gravity of the situation grew apparent. Brock didn't storm into her office and demand she help, didn't bluster on about their troubles, yet his tight shoulders and somber expression were enough to communicate how worried he was.

"Most likely the same person stole Dillon's truck, but there's no way of knowing until we catch him. Or her, I guess. You never know." He shook his head and gazed skyward inspecting the clouds. "No idea who'd want to do that to us, but there's some serious hate involved." He headed to his pickup. "I need to run out and help Cash bring the cattle in by the barn before the snow starts; they're fore-casting several inches. Can you tell Dillon to call when he's released and I'll come back to give him a ride?"

"I can take him home." She bit her tongue before she could make any other foolish offers. But Dillon hadn't mentioned anything about the vandalism. Of course not. He was no longer her client.

"Thank you again, Elle." With a final nod, he climbed into the cab and left.

She glanced up at the clouds. She should've paid more attention to the weather on the news the previous night, or at least not slept through it. Brock had mentioned several inches. Better help Dillon out before the roads got too messy.

After she got into her car, she called Betsy and left her friend severely disappointed. Elle did some fancy talking to get out of telling Betsy why she couldn't make it. Said her dad called and he'd had a bad day with his pain and was homesick.

She drove to the law enforcement center, parked, and sat for a minute wondering what to say. Dillon wasn't a guy most women would be ashamed about telling the world they brought home. In another life, she wouldn't have been either. But her job...

Technically, he was a former client. Squaring her shoulders, she walked in.

CHAPTER 10

Dillon leaned his head against the concrete wall. The morning started out rolling downhill and gained momentum as the day progressed.

He and Brock had called Aaron to check their places out to see if anything was tampered with.

The footprints at Brock's place were smaller than the previous set at Dillon's. Random incident or connected, they hadn't had time to dwell on it. Both he and Brock had gotten wrapped up in tractor shopping, taking pictures, writing down details, and getting demonstrations of their GPS systems and how they could maximize productivity. Afterward, they'd grabbed a late lunch and went to the bar to grab his truck.

Only to find it gone.

They'd reported it missing and Dillon was asked to come into the station.

He was in deep-sucking shit if he didn't spill who he was with last night. So much risk to everything he worked for, his cousins worked for; the legal fallout could be brutal. The campground owner was angry—rightly so—and he wanted

Dillon's head impaled on the splintered wood left behind from his truck's damage.

Dillon commiserated. He dreamed of doing the same to the person who'd stolen his truck.

Elle couldn't get drawn into this business. He and his cousins would work it out; he was innocent, after all.

The officer who'd been working his case approached the holding area. "There's a woman who's way out of your league telling us that you were with her during the time your truck plowed the campground. Want to tell me about it?"

"Elle?"

Dammit, Brock. He hoped his cousin had at least been discreet and called instead of barging into her office. Brock wasn't one to storm in anywhere, but he was known to be blunt.

Officer Johnson nodded. "That's her name."

Dillon's head fell back against the wall. "She was just helping me out. I had too many to go home and she let me use her spare bedroom."

"Why didn't you tell us that in the first place?"

"It was bad enough being rescued by her once. Twice in one day and I'd need to seriously find my balls." *And I'm innocent.*

Officer Johnson snorted.

"Well, the lawyer and I are leaning toward believing her over the girl who swore you left the bar drunk but keeps giving us different times."

"She was a little bitter that'd I rather sleep in my cold truck than go home with her."

The officer chuckled. "You Walker boys keep it interesting around here. We've got some paperwork for you before Ms. Brady gives you a lift home."

Another ride. Where was Brock? His ranking in Elle's eyes had to be plummeting.

He followed Officer Johnson out and filled out all the forms they set in front of him and then went out to find Elle sitting pensively in a chair, her leg crossed and bobbing furiously.

"Hey," he said.

Movement stopped and she looked up. He shifted and shoved his hands into his jacket pockets. He cared about her, about what she thought. After putting him up for the night, this seemed way worse.

"Hey," she replied, standing up. "Brock had to help Cash with some cows, so I thought I'd save him a trip back to town and take you home."

"Elle—"

"I'm parked right out front." She scurried out before he could apologize, or hell, say anything.

Outside, big fluffy snowflakes brushed his face. He settled his ball cap on his head. Good thing Brock helped Cash prep the ranch in case the snow caused problems. They'd learned to never trust an April snowfall. It could be heavy and wet and muck everything up, or it could be all that and pile up high. Or even turn into a nasty blizzard that caught people off guard and got them, and cattle, killed.

When he slid into the car, he faced her. She avoided looking at him and put the car in reverse to back out. He put his hand on the wheel. "Elle." She stopped and finally met his eyes. "I'm sorry. For everything." He expected to get an *it's okay*, or *happy to help*. Her gaze was carefully neutral. "What can I do?"

"Just let me take you home so I can get back to my house before the snow gets too bad."

Ouch. "All right."

She didn't speak to him unless it was to ask for directions. Once they were out on the highway, she leaned forward, like she could see through the snowflakes better that way.

"Geez, it's really coming down," she muttered.

And getting visibly heavier. "I think we'll get more than they forecasted."

Their speed got slower and slower until finally he cued her on the turn to the main road that ran past his house. She executed the turn carefully and then they both leaned forward to find the road.

Her knuckles were white on the wheel.

"It's all right," he spoke calmly. "It's a straight shot to my place. See the hunks of dirt built up on the side from the road grader?" She nodded tightly. "Stay to the left of those and you'll stay on the road."

That earned him a quick look of gratitude, then she concentrated until he pointed out the entrance to his drive. Noticeable because the trees surrounding his house were still visible, revealing the gap through the curtain of flakes. Once she pulled up in front of his garage, she relaxed her hands off the wheel and breathed a sigh of relief.

He hated to break the bad news to her. Undesirable news wasn't how he thought of it. More like a gift from the heavens so he could make things right. But she wouldn't see it that way.

"Elle, you can't drive home."

"Of course I can. I'll follow my tracks back to the highway."

He pointed behind them, to where her taillights high-lighted the snow behind them. "It's been less than a minute and you'd have a tough time getting out of the driveway alone."

The stages of grief played out across her face. He started to chuckle.

"This isn't funny, Dillon."

"It's kinda funny, Elle. Not you being stranded, but I can see your brain frantically searching for a way out. Look, we both know the roads are too dangerous for you to go back to town. Let me help you out this time. You can use my roof for the night. I'll even feed you." *Thank you, Mama, for the food.*

"I don't have anything with me."

He gave her a playful *tsk, tsk, tsk.* "Always keep a winter kit in your car, Doc. Most of us keep it year-round."

Distraught turned to disgruntled. "I *have* a kit, with food, blankets, and a shovel. I *don't* have clothing or toiletries."

"You can borrow a shirt and shorts and I even have a brand-new toothbrush. Come on, I don't bite." He gave her an encouraging smile and hopped out before she could argue. Before he shut the door, he turned back. "I'm going to open the garage. There's space inside for your car."

She couldn't stay. There had to be some way to get back to town. She had to work in the morning. No *way* could she explain being snowed in when she lived in town.

Watching Dillon in the glow of her headlights did not make her feel better. His piercing blue eyes on her, and his body in the spotlight. He waited patiently by the garage entrance. Even if his vehicle had been parked inside, it was still big enough to fit her car.

With great effort, she pulled her foot off the brake and eased the car inside. The garage door shut her in with the most dangerous male to her good sense. She stared in front of her at a remarkably neat and tidy workbench and her first thought was what a nice house he had. She'd expected an old farmhouse like what she passed in much of rural Minnesota, but his was newer, within the last twenty years, probably.

Her door opened and she jumped, earning her another grin on that chiseled face.

"It'll be fine, Elle. If the snow doesn't let up, it'll shut down the whole county. No one has to know you're here."

To save face and pretend that spending another night—a sober one this time—under the same roof as Dillon didn't terrify her, she told him what she'd been thinking. "Your house is more modern than I expected."

"Mom and Dad lived in a manufactured home until after I was born. Then they planned and saved for a larger home. I thought they'd die here, but Dad's illness made them want to be closer to modern amenities and they moved to Sioux Falls. Now it's mine. My aunts and uncles figured life was short. The guys live in the houses they grew up in, too."

Elle trailed him inside. "What are you all going to do when you get older?"

"Take a gamble that one of our kids will want to run the place." He shrugged off his jacket and held his hand out for hers.

"If any of my future kids help out, it'll be enough to sneak away for a weekend."

"Are you seriously that tied to the place?"

He toed off his boots and she did the same with her shoes, extremely glad she'd chosen slacks instead of a skirt. The idea of wearing his clothing didn't make her feel better. Covered in his scent, cloth that had touched his skin… No, not a good idea. A girl only had so much self-discipline, and she was completely out of her element.

"Not always. We can take off here and there. We have to, otherwise the burnout rate would be too high. There's always something to do and during some months of the year, getting the work done is more important than anything."

Dillon hung their jackets up in a closet, tossed his hat up on the shelf inside, and beckoned her farther into the dark house.

Her heart rate rose, and she wished she could run back to

her car and the security of her own home. There was no turning back. Her car was probably blocked into the garage by piling snow.

She followed him through a tidy breezeway, into the kitchen. Dillon riffled through the freezer of his fridge.

"Score." He withdrew holding a small tray covered in aluminum foil. "Mama stocked this baby the last time she was here. I can throw this in and we'll have food in forty minutes."

"From frozen to table, huh," she chuckled nervously. God, she felt like she was on a blind date. Instead of a neutral setting where she could make an escape, she was in his *freaking home.*

"She hates wasting food, so she always makes enough for one, plus leftovers for at least another meal." Turning some knobs on the oven, he tossed the tray inside, and set the timer.

Her eyes stayed on the oven for a few frantic heartbeats before she glanced up to see him staring at her. She shifted on her bare feet, at a loss for what to do.

"It's all right, Elle." He seemed to tell her that a lot. And she found she believed him. "You've risked a lot for me in the last twenty-four hours. You're safe here."

She swallowed and nodded gratefully. If he made any advances, she doubted she'd be strong enough to back away. Not after the kiss the other night.

"Let me show you the guest room and the rest of the house. Then I'll grab some of my clothes for you to use tonight."

Her feet hit the carpet, and it was so soft, she wanted to stop and scrunch her toes in it. The carpet wasn't special in itself, but the neutral tones on the walls, mixed with simple artwork and a smattering of family photos made the entire house inviting, comfortable.

Dillon had already stopped by a room, but she slowed to look at a large photograph on the wall. There were a ton of people in the picture. What would it be like to live with a family this big?

He came up beside her and pointed out individuals. "The five of us running the ranch are all in the back. Our parents are sitting in front of us and the rest of the cousins are on the ground in front of them."

Betsy couldn't have been any more accurate. The Walker Five were some good-looking men. "This was taken recently, then?"

"Two summers ago, when we learned Dad was sick." He pointed out his dad, an older version of him, who was sitting next to a pretty woman with auburn hair, Dillon's mom. "You met Brock. This is Cash." The man resembled Dillon, but with sandy brown hair and a natural mischievous tilt to his smile. "Then there's Aaron and Travis."

Travis had coffee-brown hair and blue eyes, while Aaron looked like the only blond. All five men definitely came from the same family.

"You're an only child, right?"

A sad smile highlighted his face. "Yes. Mama always joked I destroyed the place on my way out, like a rock star's hotel room. She started bleeding after I was born. They couldn't stop it, and she had to have a hysterectomy."

"I'm sorry." A single child, but with a huge family.

"With nine cousins, it's not like I grew up lonely. I didn't feel like an only child. More like I had four fraternal twins."

She marveled at how differently they'd grown up: quintessential Midwest farm boy versus city girl from the broken home.

"Who belongs to who?" she asked before she teared up at the thought of how idyllic it must've been. How it must've been what she'd always dreamed of instead of the neglectful mess she'd grown up with.

Dillon named his other cousins and what family they'd come from. She'd never remember, but she enjoyed witnessing his face animate as he added in quirks about each individual's personality.

"That's my crazy kin," he wrapped up. "I'll test you on their names later."

Her smile was genuine, the first one she'd had in several hours. Honestly, after work was done and she bid her coworkers farewell, smiling wasn't a common occurrence.

His look shuttered and he turned away. "Here's your bed for the night. Across the hall is the bathroom. You'll have it all to yourself. The master at the end of the hall has one. Mama made me move into it after they moved out. Otherwise, I planned to stay in my own room because it just felt too weird. Have a look around, while I grab some clothes."

After he cleared the doorway and his strong form strode down the hallway, she went into the room. Neat. Tidy. She suspected that no matter where she went on his property, nothing would be in disarray. Her inner therapist analyzed, assumed that he drank to gloss over a messy point in his life, rigidly making the rest of his environment simplified and organized.

Or maybe, his mom arranged everything and he was too busy, or lacked interest, to do anything differently. Or his Army habits crossed into civilian life. Damn, she had to quit doing this. He was no longer her patient.

"Will these do?"

She jumped and he chuckled. Scowling, she grabbed the shorts and shirt from him. "Thank you."

"Anytime, Elle."

She wished he would quit saying her name or go back to

calling her Doc. He infused so much intimacy into her name, made it too personal.

"Is there an extra toothbrush and comb in the bathroom?" She didn't really care, but it'd distract her from how her hormones were ignoring her brain.

"Yep. Check it out. I'll go set the table."

She was relieved when he left, and regretful. The room lost a hint of its welcome without him in it.

She clutched the clothes tightly to her chest. It's been just her for so long that Dillon taking care of her unsettled her. She'd relied on his solid confidence when she had been driving because she'd been terrified. The highway had been disappearing and she had barely seen anything through the light-speed effect of the falling snow in a moving vehicle. Then she'd turned onto the gravel and her heart stopped. There'd been nothing but a mound of white that stretched above the ditches in the beam of her headlights, the only indication that there was a road underneath the blanket of snow.

She didn't think one muscle had twitched in worry on Dillon. He'd guided her to his place, parked her in his garage, and was keeping her overnight. Like, no big.

To her it was big. It was Dillon Walker and he was meeting her needs. Her inner counselor told her to run, but the weather laughed at the notion.

She crossed the hall into the bathroom, so she could hyperventilate in private.

CHAPTER 11

Elle Brady was in his house.

She was staying overnight.

And he had to be good, be the gentlemen his mama threatened him he'd better be, because if she heard otherwise... He didn't know what would happen, but he'd never wanted to find out.

He would be honorable, too. He'd feed her, make sure she was comfortable in the guest room, then in the morning, he'd clear snow and see she got back to town safely. He owed her at least that. She damn near vibrated from her nerves. The only time she'd relaxed was when he was talking about his family. Broaching the subject that the road to the highway may not get cleared right away didn't seem like the right thing to do. He'd wait until morning. After he spent an hour clearing his drive. That was after an hour clearing a path to his shop.

The oven beeped and he took out the hot dish. He didn't know the name of it, just knew it contained most of the food groups because his mom knew him. He packed his lunch, but ate the other meals as he fit them in and food prep wasn't a high priority for him.

It smelled amazing and his stomach growled in agreement. He laid it on the counter and went about getting plates and silverware. It came as no surprise that he liked setting his little used dining table for two, instead of being one lonely bastard eating straight from the aluminum foil pan.

A quick perusal of his fridge revealed that water was the only other choice than beer and milk. Given he'd been chowing leftovers in the mornings, it'd be better to put beer in his next bowl of cereal than take a gamble on that milk. The state of his food supply was normally sad, but with Elle under his roof, it dawned on him how pitiful it really was.

He'd have to remedy that.

He wondered if she'd come out of the bathroom willingly, or if he'd have to coax her out like a skittish mare.

She appeared at the table, wearing her work outfit. No surprise. If he took a wager on whether she'd change clothes to sleep, he'd probably lose.

"Smells delicious."

"Mama can't make a bad dish, I swear. Go ahead and eat."

Her mouth quirked. "I like how you call her mama. It seems so Southern, but you're so not."

He dug into his food. "When you have ten kids running around hollering 'mom,' it can be hard to get the right mom's attention. So I started with mama. I think it made her feel like the queen over my aunts."

Elle chuckled, an enchanting sound reminiscent of Gram's wind chimes. She didn't laugh enough. Was it due to her career or the unknown story with her dad?

"Is your father the oldest?" She sat and began to eat.

"Yes, and I'm the oldest cousin, too. He and my uncles were all older before they got married, but once one did, they fell like dominos. Mama was the first to get pregnant then it was like something was in the water. Cash showed up a month after me, then Travis, Brock, and Aaron."

"That's so cool." She sounded wistful.

"What about your family?"

It was like the food in her mouth turned into a wet paper towel, but she finished chewing before she spoke. "My mom left when I was thirteen. And you know about my dad."

Not really, and he guessed it was a diversionary tactic to not have to talk about him. His mom and aunts and uncles were all living the life, halfway retired and doing things they couldn't do while working the land full-time. Elle's dad was already in assisted living.

"What happened, Elle?" he asked softly.

Her beautiful emerald eyes dimmed. "I told you how he fell."

"I mean before that. Why's a young guy like your dad hanging out with my grandma?"

"Oh." She pushed her hair behind her ear and twirled her fork around in her food. He got the feeling he would get the abridged version. "He's had…health problems much of my life. Then he developed leukemia and the treatment made him so weak."

"And there's just you?"

"Just me," she echoed, and took a bite. To keep from having to talk about herself?

"No siblings or cousins?" he pressed.

She shook her head. "Only child, and not many cousins. They didn't live nearby; I never got to know them."

Dillon sat back, done with his food. He couldn't imagine growing up without family invading every facet of his life. He'd grown up with cousins, gone to school with them, graduated with them, gone into business with them. Then there had been him and Cash. They'd been like twins. Would they ever reconcile? Not when Cash remained oblivious to how utterly upset and disappointed Dillon was in him.

He scrubbed his face, suddenly tired. It'd been a long day after a night with little sleep. "Sometimes they can be my biggest headaches."

She gave him a small smile. "You're very fortunate to be surrounded by a support network."

"I know. We're a little more spread out than we used to be, but…" He shrugged. "I remember wanting to get away so bad. Everyone lived in Moore, so it was like we never traveled anywhere. I love where I came from, but I just wanted," his lips quirked, "more than Moore."

Elle's soft laugh rippled straight through him like a ray of sunshine. He loved making that serious face of hers break into a sweet smile.

"But," he continued, "after I grew up, I realized how good I had it here, and that it's what I want in life."

She was watching him, and he couldn't fathom what was going on in that sharp mind of hers.

"But you're not happy."

He opened his mouth to argue, then closed it. She wasn't wrong. "I'm content." He was way more content with her here.

"If that were true, you wouldn't have come to my office."

"I told you why I was there."

He got the *really?* stare. "You have some feelings you're not dealing with. That's why those who love you are worried about you."

"Is this session number three, Doc?"

She didn't leave the table, or get irritated at his cavalier remark. She faced him fully. "You're not my client anymore."

He leaned over the table, hating that the plank of wood was in his way. "Then what am I?"

No answer immediately spilled from her. They could be called friends, but he didn't want to stop there.

"You're someone I'm concerned about. You should finish out your sessions with another counselor."

"I'm not going to go to another counselor, Elle."

"Then I still recommend AA. At least give it a try."

Ugh, he didn't want to have this talk. Going to Fargo every week to sit in a room didn't entice him. He waved for her to stay seated while he cleared their plates. Laying the dishes on the counter, his gaze rose to the window and the steady fall of fat, white flakes. Even if he'd wanted to, there'd be no getting out for any meeting.

"I'll think about it." He wouldn't. "We don't have to worry about going anywhere tonight. Or tomorrow it looks like."

"I have to work tomorrow." Elle popped up and rushed to the window. "Look at all that snow!"

"I doubt anything in town will be open tomorrow. This stuff'll melt fast, but we'll be plugged in for a day or two." Then it'd be a sloppy mess to get to the highway, but he wasn't going to mention that, nor how poorly her car would handle the muck.

An unusual chiming sound filtered into the kitchen.

"My phone!" Elle ran back to the guest room.

Her departure left the kitchen too quiet. He really liked having her around, in his home. Her voice drifted in. She must've caught the caller in time. Cleaning up, he rushed to finish before she ended her conversation so she wouldn't feel pressured to help.

With just him, he rarely ran the dishwasher. The appliance was used when he had company and that was usually his mom, and only when she embarked on her cooking extravaganzas. He washed the dishes, cleaned up the table, and put the leftovers in the fridge. It'd be enough to serve one more meal—and help hide the beer.

He stood with the fridge door open, thinking about putting some of the beer in a cupboard because it made the lack of other food really noticeable. No, that would mean he had something to hide. A young bachelor with beer in the fridge was nothing unusual.

Yet he quickly shut the door when Elle walked back in. No reason, other than the door was blocking his view of her incredible body.

She glanced around and saw everything had been cleaned up. "Oh. Thanks for picking up and for dinner. I think I'm going to head to bed."

Shoving his hands into his pockets, he cocked his head toward the living room. "Are you sure you don't want to join me for an exciting night of watching the news and weather?"

Despite her almost tangible effort to keep him at a distance, she smiled. "I'll leave it all to you." Her eyes danced over his chest, then back up to his face; she flushed at his focused gaze. "Good night Dillon."

"'Night Elle."

Flustered, she turned to go back to her room.

After suppressing a frustrated sigh, he flopped on the couch and grabbed the remote because he hadn't been joking about his plans.

ELLE'S EYES FLIPPED OPEN. The room was dark. She peeked at her phone. Two in the morning. She'd gotten a few hours of sleep after assuring her dad she was okay when he'd called, omitting the fact that she wasn't at home.

She'd been fast asleep when Dillon had gone to bed. So what woke her?

A muffled groan. Frowning, she crawled out of bed and tiptoed to the closed door.

There it was again. It sounded like Dillon was talking to someone, only it came in short spurts interspersed with moans.

She crept out of the room and followed the noise to the end of the house toward the master bedroom. His door was ajar. Shadows filled the room, making it hard to see his large form on the bed, twisting in the sheets.

He was having a nightmare.

More incoherent mumbling in a tortured voice. She just couldn't go back to her room and let him play out the episode on his own.

"Dillon," she called.

He flopped to his other side, the dream's hold on him too strong. "Cash, fall back, dammit."

He was so frantic; her instinct to comfort kicked in. She took a step forward, hesitated. It wasn't her place. But when he wrenched like he was in pain, she rushed over to his side.

"Dillon," she said softly. She called again, but louder, not wanting to startle him and put herself into danger.

He stilled. His eyes flew open, then he sat up. When he blinked and looked around, she stepped closer but didn't touch him. He hadn't been diagnosed with PTSD, but he was obviously having a nightmare. She wouldn't march over and wake up anyone stuck in a bad dream.

"Dillon," she said, louder. When he blinked and looked around, she laid a hand on his shoulder.

"You scared me," he said and angled toward her, putting a hand on her waist.

Too late, she realized she hadn't thrown his loaned shorts on and was in Dillon's bedroom in only a T-shirt and panties.

He peered up at her. "What's wrong?"

"It's not me. I think you were having a bad dream."

His other hand settled on her waist, pulling her close. She

resisted, but feared she'd lose her balance and topple onto him.

Her body thought him catching her was a good idea.

In one swift motion, he pulled her down to him and rolled on top of her across his king-size bed.

Before she could get a rational argument out about how she couldn't do this, his lips crashed down on hers.

Her body won, forcing her brain to submit to the pleasure of his heavy body anchoring her own. His tongue swept inside to tangle with hers. Her legs moved of their own volition until she cradled his big frame, his arousal pressing into her.

Tilting her hips, she wanted his length to stroke her where she grew wet for him. Her body didn't require much encouragement around Dillon.

A moan of pleasure escaped from them both. He propped himself on one arm, still kissing her deeply, but pulled her shirt up with his free hand.

She bowed into him as he cupped her breast, massaging, rolling the nipple between his fingers. She continued to rock her hips into him, frustrated by the underwear they both wore.

She gently scored him with her nails as her hands skimmed down his back.

His tongue swirled around hers and his hand left her breast to trail down her abdomen.

God, yes.

When he slipped under her panties, she reared back to cry in relief, but he was intent on keeping them connected, as if afraid she'd run if he let her go. With their kiss in place, he found her clit and stroked a smooth circle; she almost flew apart. It'd been too long.

He stroked and flicked, and while she missed his erection teasing her, the orgasm his fingers promised more than made up for it. Then he entered her, sliding one long, capable digit inside.

She groaned into his mouth, nipping his tongue. Her hands gripped his shoulders and he set a steady pace, stroking in tandem with his finger while his thumb circled her nub. She rolled her hips, seeking the explosive end.

Pressure built, oxygen was limited as she panted against his mouth. Breaking the kiss, she flung her head back into the blankets to cry out.

"Dillon!"

"That's it, Elle. Honey, you're so wet, just dripping for me. I want to do this with my tongue. I want to taste every. Inch. Of you."

The words were so unlike anything she'd heard from him, yet they framed the most erotic experience she'd had. In the shadows, the strain in his face from holding back was visible. He watched where they were connected, where he worked her into a frenzy. Her legs parted wide, his body settled between—it sent her over the edge.

She bowed back, flooding his hand with her release.

"Let it go," he growled. "Let me give you this."

His voice, his commands, she cried his name over and over, quaking around him. After she was over the crest, he continued working her, until she weakly pushed against him unsure she could take anymore.

His slid his finger out, making her shudder again. Cool air wafted over her heated skin as he skated one side of her panties down, maneuvering it off one leg. Her leg fell to the side, leaving her open to him.

Shoving his own underwear down, he placed himself at her entrance, the broad head of his silky erection slowly pushing in.

When she realized why it felt so divine, she gasped. "Dillon. Protection."

He swore and pulled back. "I'm sorry, Elle. I wasn't thinking. You're driving me outta my ever-lovin' mind." He dropped his forehead down to hers, then gave her a sweet kiss. "I'll go grab a condom."

"Dillon…" Her rational mind was returning, and other than being pleased that he didn't keep a huge stash by his bed for randoms he brought home, sex with Dillon would be an event she couldn't walk away from. Him getting her off in the dark seemed a little less…binding. "We shouldn't do this."

Releasing a heavy sigh, he straightened and pulled his boxer briefs up. "You're killing me, woman."

She scooted back to search for her panties, which had finally fallen off completely. They eluded her as she pawed around the sheets. The scrap of fabric held the appeal of a suit of armor, encasing the raw emotions coursing through her body while she wondered, what now?

He yanked the covers back before she could scurry back to her room. Rolling her in next to him, still sans panties, he covered them with the blankets.

His strong embrace holding her gently in place, the bed warm and inviting, this was a bad idea. "I don't think—"

"Just stay for tonight." He nuzzled her hair, murmuring into her ear. "Keep the memories away, so all I remember is how you looked coming in my arms."

Her cheeks flushed hot. Memories gave him nightmares, and he wanted to override them with her orgasming wantonly as he gazed on. If he'd have professed his vulnerability to anyone else, she would've said no, it wasn't a problem.

Nightmares, flashbacks, were serious business and he had shoved them aside, seeking comfort in her. Just like she had in his embrace, in the care he took of her, because her lonely existence had been overwhelming lately.

But it'd happened. And here they were. The barren bed in

the other room held no appeal. Not when they both sought solace in the other.

She turned into him and cuddled into his body, loving his muscles wrapped around her. The only thing making it slightly uncomfortable was the protruding erection tenting his underwear, poking her in the stomach.

She lightly kissed him on the shoulder her head was tucked against. "Are you going to be able to sleep with that thing?"

"Eventually."

Biting her lip, she attempted to talk sense into herself about what she was going to do. Hadn't she just lectured herself on the seriousness of the situation?

But tonight, she was just a woman being intimate with a man. In the darkness of the bedroom, she wanted to believe they were any normal couple and the issues between them could wait until morning.

The languid, relaxation in her own muscles guided her hand. She freed his shaft and wrapped her hand around him.

He hissed in a breath. "You don't have to do that."

Instead of just a kiss, she grazed his skin with her teeth. "I want to."

He shifted to crook one leg, giving her more room to work him. Velvet steel flowed under her hand; she squeezed and let up to create a rippling sensation of pleasure moving over his cock. He pushed into her, his breaths coming quicker, his body tensing.

To drive him as out of his mind as he'd driven her, she licked and kissed his chest, pumping her hand faster and faster.

"God, Elle. That's amazing," he gasped. "Yeah, squeeze harder."

He gave a long groan, throwing his head back, angling his pelvis into her. He swelled and pulsed within her grip. She hadn't thought out the logistics, but he had, grabbing her underwear and wrapping it around the tip of his shaft. Finally, he let himself come.

Bringing this man to his figurative knees with one hand—empowering. It was almost, *almost*, worth missing the ecstasy of him driving himself inside of her.

"I grabbed it off the covers when I tucked us in. I didn't want you to do something foolish like put it back on." He was breathless, but smug.

"I still have your shirt on."

"Don't remind me, or you'll find yourself with another request for the use of your hand again."

She giggled and stayed curled up with him, eventually falling asleep in his arms.

CHAPTER 12

*D*illon woke at his normal time, but he didn't move. A lovely round bottom pressed into his side. Elle's soft breathing was something he could listen to all day.

What a night. Hands down the best of his life. Waking up to Elle standing over him, he just couldn't help it. Compounded by the shitty, recurring dream, he'd reacted and reached out for her.

The side of his mouth quirked. Her attraction rivaled his own. He got the impression she didn't let just anyone do what he did to her. She liked him and she was trying to resist. He understood, but he could also work with that.

Arm slung behind his head, a half-mast erection growing in his boxer briefs, he stared at the ceiling. There was a whole lotta snow waiting for him. He really should go out and tackle it.

Right now, this moment, he didn't want to disrupt it. Afraid that as soon as Elle roused from her slumber, the spell would be broken. She'd retreat into her mind and hold herself at a distance from him.

Every inch she placed between them would serve to

remind him of the shameless way she'd broken apart. Her silhouette had been like a beacon, with her luminous flesh glowing in the dark. As much as he'd give his left nut to see the shade her skin flushed from orgasm in broad daylight, he knew she wasn't there yet. His hold on her was too tenuous.

And he wanted to hold onto her.

Gaining her trust meant not pushing her too fast. So instead of learning every nuance of her body, he'd go out and fire up the smaller tractor that he'd, thankfully, kept the bucket on for pushing snow.

But *day-um*, he didn't want to leave the bed. Paradise.

With a groan, he rolled over and lifted her unbelievably soft flaxen hair to kiss the nape of her neck.

This was going to end one of two ways. She'd either come awake with a gasp, becoming more dismayed when she remembered she still wore no underwear. Then using the blankets as a shield, she'd slide out of the other side of the bed and scurry to the shower holding his shirt tightly around her.

Or, she'd smile as her eyelids fluttered open, maybe stretch back into him, unwilling to regret for one moment what they'd done together.

"What time is it?" she asked in a sleep-heavy voice.

"Early yet, but I gotta go out and move a ton of snow."

"How much did we get?" She relaxed in his arms and snow was the last thing he wanted to be pushing.

Because he remembered how her wet, tight entrance had felt on his cock...aaand he was back at painful erection stage.

"Dunno. You'll be the first one I tell after I measure." He kept his nose buried in her hair. If he did anything else, he wouldn't be able to keep himself from exploring between her long legs. "Help yourself to whatever you need or stay in bed all morning, whatever you want."

He rubbed her bare hip, dangerously close to the flesh he

wanted to sink his fingers into. Giving her ass cheek a couple of taps, enjoying her inhale of surprise, he rolled back to his side of the bed to get out.

He snagged his clothes from the top of his dresser and glanced back at her before he went to the master bathroom. She peeked out at him from under the mess of her gorgeous hair and blankets. She didn't look regretful, or like she wanted to escape, she looked like she wanted exactly what he did.

Flashing her a wicked grin that made her blush, he closed the door to get cleaned up.

ELLE STOOD in front of the mirror wondering what the hell she'd gotten herself into. Dillon's gray Moore High School football shirt hung off her shoulders. It was the only scrap of cloth on her body and she didn't want to take it off.

With some embarrassment, she wondered where her underwear was. Wherever it lay after last night, it wasn't wearable.

Exasperated at herself, she pulled his shirt off and folded it to lay on the counter. Then she searched through the cabinets to find a brush. She usually wore minimal makeup, and she wished she had stashed some in her purse, but today would be au naturel.

Years of swimming helped her grow comfortable with her body. Strutting around the pool for hours in nothing but a swimsuit that covered only her bits and pieces gave a girl a solid sense of self. Pool water was hell on even waterproof makeup, so she'd only worn it to give her a more mature appearance, even when her college swim days were over. Otherwise, her twenty-seven-year-old professional self appeared barely old enough to drink.

Once she was done freshening up, she headed to the kitchen. The house was empty and scraping sounds came from outside. She peered out the window. Dillon shoveled a path to an extremely large shop. He wore only a hooded sweatshirt over tan coveralls, heavy boots, and of course, a baseball hat.

The hat was yellow and grungy. She smiled. Like women had different purses for different occasions, farm boys had different hats.

He attacked the cold, wet, heavy snow. A lot of it. It would take hours to clear the area between his shop and the garage, then the driveway. She didn't see any drifts. With the bright sun, all the tall trees that surrounded his place were on display. No idea they were that plentiful. Last night, they'd been towering shadows behind the snowfall. The property his house actually sat on was completely surrounded, like its own little oasis amidst farmland. Had there been wind, drifting might not have been a huge issue, anyway. Mature evergreens and cottonwoods formed a ring of protection.

Dillon disappeared into the shop. She recalled the vandalism he'd told her about and wondered who'd want to threaten all of this. Or Dillon.

She sighed and turned away. He fed her, cleaned up, gave her the distance she needed. Even when she carried things farther than planned, he'd respected her wishes to not go all the way. Although, if he'd had protection within immediate proximity, she doubted she would've stopped him. Regretting not experiencing everything Dillon had to offer her body, she sported the feminine equivalent of blue balls.

She opened the fridge and deduced that breakfast would not be found there. Silver cans of beer lined both shelves, with some ketchup in the door. She scanned the kitchen. No dead silver bullets littered the counter or lay in the garbage. Unless he hid them, but she didn't think so.

He might not think he had a problem, but there were unresolved issues that had come home with him from the Army. The lack of photos from his military days suggested that. Family photos covered the walls, but no pictures of graduation from basic training, nothing of his military buddies, and none from his time overseas.

One of the guys she'd dated in college had been in the Army and his apartment had been covered in the evidence. He'd had portraits of soldiers in uniform, group shots of soldiers-gone-wild at the strip clubs, and albums of his time overseas. Those were physical examples. Their conversations had been peppered with his time in the military. *You can take the soldier out of the Army, but you can't take the Army out of the soldier.*

It was like Dillon erased his time away from the farm, regretted leaving at all.

Gone for eight years. That's almost halfway to military retirement. And then he'd come home and his father had gotten sick and passed away. Was he guilt-ridden, like he'd chosen to spend eight years away from the man who'd meant the most to him in the world?

Elle rummaged through a few cupboards and found some Pop-Tarts. She grabbed a packet to munch on while she finished pondering the man who'd centered himself in her world.

She liked him. A lot.

She migrated to the window where she squinted through the large sliding door into the shop. Jeepers, the building was huge, resembled a small airplane hangar. Rumblings of a tractor came from inside. Out rolled an older red tractor with a scoop bucket on the front. Dillon sat behind the wheel, running the bucket as he started the tedious process of clearing snow.

He looked so natural, could probably run that thing in his

sleep. Occasionally, he'd lean over each side, but his focus was on the snow, moving it around like he'd probably done his whole life.

Well, she was a Minnesota girl. She'd run a shovel her whole life, so she could help, too.

She couldn't shovel in her work clothes from the day before or in the shoes she'd worn. The trunk of her car held the answer.

It was a mad dash to find the lights in the garage, rush across the cold floor in her bare feet, and pop the trunk. Inside, she had snow pants and boots, still packed from her trip to the Twin Cities the previous month.

She dressed and punched the garage door opener. As it rose, the drone of the tractor grew louder. A snow shovel hung in a rack on the wall, easy to spot as they were lined up tidy. The first job she tackled was the wall of snow the garage door had been holding back. The snow must be at least a foot and a half high, threatening to spill into the garage.

If the roads had this amount, there was little chance her car was going to make it.

She started at the top and cut her way down, opening a swath in front of the garage for Dillon to maneuver in close with the bucket. At one point, she looked up to see him give her an easy nod and smile.

The strong rays of the sun ate away at the mass accumulation of sparkling crystals, but the massive amount would take a few days to melt entirely, if the temps stayed up.

While Dillon labored on opening the driveway to the road, she shoveled around the house, tromping through wet snow to her knees, listening as it melted and trickled down the gutters from the roof.

The tractor lumbered back, aiming for the shop.

She trekked in after him. After the intense shine outside, her eyes worked to adjust to the dimness.

When her gaze landed on the large red tractor marred by poorly matching blotches of spray paint, she wandered closer. So this was what Brock had been talking about.

"It's bad, but it's all superficial." Dillon came up beside her, and she tried not to lose herself in thoughts of how right this felt.

"I guess no one's looking when you're out in the field, but it's just so awful."

"I know," he said grimly. "It's an old model anyway, so we've decided to upgrade. The last few years have been good ones, not too wet, not too dry, no hail storms. We're sitting comfortably enough to upgrade. I'm just glad he didn't hurt anyone when he stole my truck."

"No idea who it is?"

"It's a small town, but no one's heard anything. I've no idea why us. Why *my* property has been the only one touched."

"Your cousins haven't had problems?"

Dillon shook his head. "Brock said he thought maybe someone had been out to his place, but the others haven't experienced anything unusual. I'm the closest to town." He pointed to the south. "Cash and the ranch portion of our business are over there." Then he pointed east. "As you drive down the road, Brock's place is the next one on this side of the road. Then Aaron, and Travis lives at the dead end."

"Five farming bachelors all in a line?"

His blue eyes crinkled with humor. "Well, Travis has had a girlfriend since college. Fiancée, actually. They got engaged last summer."

His tone was so neutral, not animated like when he talked about the rest of his family. "You don't like her?"

She got a noncommittal shrug. "It's not that I don't like her, it's just that she... He deserves someone's who's a little more excited about our way of life. She's always running to the cities for shopping and going out with friends, hardly ever comes to our gatherings, lives in town even though he's asked her to move in." He shrugged again. "He loves her, so whatever."

He fell quiet and rubbed the back of his neck. Only sounds of water dripping off the tractor as snow melted filled the large shop. She sensed Dillon wasn't telling her something.

"What is it?"

"I didn't see any signs of the plows on the main road. It's melting rapidly, but not fast enough to take off fifteen inches of fresh powder. Sorry, Elle. I think you're stuck here another day."

Yeah, she should be sorry, too. Summoning the response was too much effort. He shuffled next to her, like he had more to add.

"It's okay. Is something wrong?"

He took his hat off to scratch his head. "Well, once it's plowed, these roads tend to be pretty sloppy for a day or two, depending on sunshine. Our pickups make it through fine, but your little car…"

She was stuck here. "Oh shit, work! I forgot to call."

"I'm sure they're closed. The news last night said all the towns in the path of the storm were shut down. Tomorrow's Friday and people are still going to be cleaning up."

Yeah, maybe. She had shelter, the only thing more important was— "Oh God, Dillon, what are we going to eat? You've got no food."

He laughed good naturedly, eyes twinkling. "My freezer's stocked and you haven't seen my emergency stash in the basement. We still have power, so no worries."

She followed him out of the shop. He pushed the doors closed and they headed inside through the garage where they both stripped out of their wet, sweaty clothes.

Ugh, she needed a shower. "Can I borrow some more clothes and throw these in the wash?"

"Sure thing. I have a few things to add to it, too." He shot her a knowing smirk.

A blush crawled up her skin. What was going to develop over the next two days alone with him?

CHAPTER 13

*E*lle was his for another day or two. Thank you, unexpected spring snowstorm. Dillon stepped out of the shower and dressed. He gathered up everything for the laundry and stopped to pick up Elle's clothes from outside the bathroom door where he told her to leave them. Setting down a pair of shorts and T-shirt, he tried not think about how she'd been commando all morning.

It'd been a losing battle while watching her bend and stomp around in her adorable winter gear. Gray snow pants had never been so sexy.

He thought she'd stay in bed or migrate back to her room after grabbing something to eat. Maybe spend the morning wandering through the house or watching TV. Then the garage door had opened and his little snow bunny had shoveled away. They made a damn good team and his male pride enjoyed her car in his garage.

Dropping the laundry in the wash, he spotted her bra in the pile. Good God, he wasn't going to survive if she went braless and panty-less around his house.

He punched the buttons of the machine, then stopped to

brace himself against it. He heard her coming out of the bathroom, where he'd see her in his clothes, wearing nothing underneath. Lust licked through his body, settling—along with his blood supply—in his groin.

They needed to eat. He could distract himself by feeding her.

One of Mama's meals sounded good. Better than his emergency stash of canned goods. Digging through the freezer, he found some of her homemade tomato soup. As long as his cheese and bread hadn't gone bad, he'd whip up some grilled cheese.

"Dillon," Elle called from her room, "can I borrow a sweatshirt, too?"

"Yeah, take a look around my room. There's one hanging somewhere."

The soup was melting in the pot and he had a few sandwiches ready to fry when she walked out in an old Army sweatshirt. Leave it to her to find his stash of Army pride clothing that he never wore anymore. The wet hair and makeup free face made her look young and enchanting.

He shot her a smile. "Hungry?"

"Smells delicious. Is that homemade?"

"Soup by Mama, grilled cheese by me. Nothing but the best for you," he said with a grin.

Elle pitched in to help because that's what she did. She obviously wasn't one to stand by and watch, be waited on. Must be what she'd had to do when her mom left, then when her dad got sick.

No family, but at least Elle still had Gary. Being surrounded by family was one of the main reasons why he came back home. Cash and his epic fuckup was the other.

They sat down at the table with their spread. From the way they both dug into it with glee, lunch hit the spot.

"So now what?" Elle took the dishes to the sink and to

wash them. "What do farmers and ranchers do when it's a snow day for everyone else?"

"Bachelor farmers clean house, but mine's still pretty good. That leaves tinkering in the shop. There's always something to do. However, I have company, so I'm calling it a snow day."

She paused and looked over her shoulder. "Don't let me stop you from your work."

"Once this mess melts, there'll be more than enough work for me. I wouldn't mind a day off." Especially one with a beautiful woman. "Really, we already worked half of it."

She chuckled as if that made her feel better, like she'd ever be a burden.

He helped her finish the dishes. Her back was to him wiping down the counter. Seizing the opportunity, he swirled his towel, winding it fast, then whipping it out to snap her in the butt.

She yelped and spun on him. The surprise in her eyes faded into cold calculation. Her hand reached into the sink, pulling up a mound of suds that she threw in his face.

Laughing, he lunged for her. She tossed one more handful before he pinned her between himself and the counter.

Her flushed expression hinted that she had the same thoughts he was having: that she was tired of the distance between them. He solved the problem with a kiss.

She greedily returned his kiss. He pushed her shorts down before lifting her out of them to the counter. Expecting resistance, he got none. To test the waters, he ran his hands up her legs, under the sweatshirt and shirt. Cupping her breasts, thumbing her nipples, her groan of approval was very satisfying to his craving. Need controlled his movements, he couldn't be accused of thinking with his dick. Since he met her, *this* was his goal, to break her out of her shell and make her his.

She hesitated only slightly before breaking the kiss to raise her arms and yank both tops off.

He couldn't breathe. Every inch, from her perfect breasts down to where she was opened to him, was on display. Under her left breast was a tattoo of a wave with the outline of a swimmer in black ink. Erotic as hell.

He traced it with his finger. "Got any more?"

"You'll have to find out. I need your shirt off."

He ripped it off in less than two seconds, unbuttoned his pants in one, freeing himself. His cock twitched, painfully responsive, even to his own touch.

"Elle," he spoke so low it was almost a whisper. "I need to be inside of you, but I've got to go find my wallet." He wanted to ask her if she was on anything, if she trusted he was clean. He'd never been in a woman without a shield between them, would've never risked it. He wanted nothing between him and Elle and he wanted her *now*.

That pink tongue of hers flicked out to lick her lips.

He groaned. "You're killing me, woman."

"Maybe I can take care of that." She eased off the counter and nudged him around until his back was toward it.

Holy shit, was she really going to—

Sinking to her knees answered his question. Yes. Yes she was.

He braced his hands on the counter behind him, his pelvis jerking when her cool hand wrapped around his length. Meeting his gaze, she licked the tip and he almost buckled to his knees, too.

She took him in her mouth and he dropped his head back. Blow jobs weren't something he experienced a lot of. One of the downsides of never really being in a relationship. When he did hook-up, it was fast and mutually pleasing, but not often did he and his partner have the time, or ambition, to explore.

Elle—he would get lost in her. Wanted to learn every inch of her delectable body, every move that made her shudder. All she needed to do was let him. This was above and beyond.

His hips moved of their own accord. Supreme effort was used to not thrust and gag her. He gripped the counter to maintain some control.

Naked, on her knees in front of him, mouth on his cock equaled ready to come, but he managed to prolong the most intense experience of his life.

Threading his fingers into her hair, he watched her take him in as far she could, her cheeks hollow as she sucked back down his length. It was too much, the sight of her pleasuring him. The orgasm refused to be held back anymore. He grabbed a towel off the counter to catch his release.

"I'm going to come." His strangled warning came just before his ejaculate exploded out of him.

But Elle kept going and he lost himself in her mouth, grunting her name, jerking his hips, one hand still buried in her hair, the other holding him up. She took him, all of him. Just when he thought it couldn't get any more arousing, she let him go and licked her lips.

Sagging against the counter, he might be spent, but he wasn't done. He wanted to rock her ever-lovin' world like she'd done to him.

"Lay back," he growled.

Lids heavy with desire, a blush of arousal highlighting her skin, she did as he asked. Broad daylight, and she was stretched out on the floor, waiting for him.

He shoved down his pants the rest of the way, got down, and spread her legs. Finding her swollen nub, he feasted on her.

She bucked and hollered his name, but he was relentless, using his tongue to drive her wild. She tasted so sweet and was close to climax. He backed off and teased her, sliding his finger in and out.

"You're destroying me, Dillon," she gasped, writhing against his face.

He nipped her, and she jumped, moaning again with pleasure. Her feet rested on his shoulders, knees fallen to the side. She was utterly at his mercy where she'd had full control of him just minutes before. Only then did he think he matched the fervor she'd created within him.

She gripped his hair while she rode him, her body wanting the release he promised. He relented, curling his finger slightly inside her.

"Omigod," she cried.

Her release was decadent. He held her, tasted her, pleasured her until she went limp, her feet falling from his shoulders.

Painfully hard again, the sight of her spent on his kitchen floor came straight out of his dreams. He crawled up her belly to stretch over her, kissing her neck while she caught her breath.

"Will you let me in, Elle? I want you so bad."

Maybe it was the sound of his desperation, maybe she needed him as badly as he did her. Whatever made her cradle him with her legs and place him at her entrance, he was grateful. His focus was slowly on pushing inside heaven. Wet, hot, and tight, still quivering from her orgasm. If she hadn't taken care of him, he would've exploded by now.

Supporting himself on his elbows, he wanted to watch her. He couldn't read the look in her eyes. Yes, there was pleasure, but there was something deeper, more serious, like she didn't know if this was a good idea, but like him, wanted it—severely.

When he was seated fully inside he stilled, letting her adjust around him. Was this what it felt like with no barriers?

Except with Elle, he could wear five condoms and she'd still feel like the softest, warmest glove on his most sensitive flesh.

Legs wrapping around his waist was a signal he needed to start stroking. Pumping his hips slowly at first, he worked them both back up, until their breaths came in pants and moans, and her legs were pulling him in just as hard as he was pushing.

He reached between them to circle her clit as he thrust, and sucked a nipple into his mouth. She raked her nails across his back, a reaction he loved from her.

He pumped into her. The spasms holding his cock so tightly finished him. Elle hollered his name and dropped her arms back on the floor and arched her back. Hair framed her head, spread out like the halo of a sex goddess. She climaxed in the sunlight, shouting her elation from an orgasm that gripped his shaft tighter than it had his fingers. He joined her wanton release with a curt shout before throwing his head back and releasing deep inside her willing body.

Collapsing on top of her, he worried he was too heavy with a hard floor sandwiching her on the other side. He rolled to the side and wrapped her in his arms.

"I know this is kind of late but," his voice was rough, raw, "are you on anything?" Oddly, it wouldn't bother him if she wasn't. He already knew she wasn't a quick fuck, that he wanted a lot more from her than her body.

She nodded against his shoulder, but didn't say anything.

He looked down at her. "Everything all right?"

She chewed her lower lip and nodded again, but still said nothing.

A crooked finger under her chin brought her gaze up to him. "It's okay, Elle. What we did wasn't wrong."

The indecision deep in her emerald eyes confirmed he nailed the problem on the head.

She sighed. "I know. It was just…unexpected. I was ready, but I wasn't."

He wanted her to feel as comfortable about this as he did, and she needed more time. "Do you like watching movies? I'm a little backlogged on my to-watch list. We could see what's available."

"That sounds nice."

"I even have popcorn we could make." He got up and held out a hand for her.

She gifted him with the sweetest smile as he helped her up and handed her his sweatshirt and shorts back.

"So what do you like—action, drama, comedy?" He'd watch whatever she requested, do damn near whatever she wanted.

WHAT ELLE WANTED WAS to have more sex with Dillon. Their tryst on the kitchen floor had busted the dam of her inhibitions.

They watched the latest superhero movie to kill the afternoon. Before the credits rolled, she gladly found herself naked on her back on the couch with him pushing inside.

They had a roast for supper—plentiful cuts of quality meats, one of the benefits of a ranch. After the dishes were done, they managed to keep their hands—mostly—off each other to watch another movie. Now she was spread on top of him, riding him like her life depended on it. It might not, but after the snow melted, and the roads were drivable, she feared this wouldn't last.

They'd each go back to their own lives and their problems would still be there. Even if he wasn't her client anymore, she didn't want to repeat her childhood, or her adult years.

He palmed her breasts, dissolving any apprehension, yet her desperation showed in her frantic pace.

Would she ever get enough? They could fuck all weekend and she'd go home and want him again, and again.

Her orgasm crashed down. Throwing her head back, crying out, she tried not to weep with her release because how much more time did she have with him before reality sunk back in?

He crested with her, his hands digging into her hips. She swayed from the effort, boneless from her own finish. Draped over him, they both caught their breath while he stroked her hair.

"Are you going to tell me what's wrong?" he murmured in her ear.

She squeezed her eyes shut, wondering how she should answer. She went with the simple truth. "I guess I'm scared."

"About us?" From the moment they met, he'd been single-minded about her. If only it was so easy for her. "Are you scared about work? I don't think you did anything wrong."

"I did if it stops you from getting help."

His solid chest became rock hard as he tensed. "I'm not seeing anyone else."

"Dillon—"

"No, Elle. It was hard enough to make the appointment with *you*. I can't go to another stranger and have them think there's something wrong with me, too."

"It's okay to admit you have a problem."

Gently, he lifted her off him and turned them to the side so they could face each other. "Have you seen me have a drink since you've been here?"

"Alcoholism doesn't work like that."

He scowled. "Is that what your textbooks told you?"

"It's what living with my father told me," she said flatly.

She pushed against his embrace, but the circle of his arms was immovable.

"Tell me about him."

She gave up, both on trying to distance herself from him and keeping her family drama a secret. "My mom left us because of his drinking. At times he was so useless, I would have to call in sick for him. In high school, I worked to put groceries on the table because he could barely keep the bills paid. I worked my ass off to afford college, spent every moment in the pool trying to earn a full-ride scholarship."

"Did you?"

"No. I earned a partial scholarship, got a few grants, but I have a shitload of loans. I worked a couple of jobs to help offset the cost and I went to school close by so I could live at home. I needed to take care of Dad anyway." She looked away, trying to blink back tears.

"Is that how he broke a hip?" Dillon asked softly.

"No, he's been in the longest stretch of sobriety I've ever witnessed. But he kinda had to quit to live, which I wasn't sure would be enough for him. He destroyed himself and developed leukemia. Never recovered his strength after chemo, and then he fell down the stairs."

A tear escaped, she allowed a few more to fall, breaking her oath to herself to never cry over this again. "Grad school was the most miserable experience of my life. I went to class, shuttled him to the hospital and back. He barely survived treatment. I still can't believe he's in remission, but... That's why I moved here. A town big enough to need an addiction counselor, but small enough I can run home to check on him at lunch. Or afford a nursing home."

"Doesn't he have a pension or something?" He swiped a tear off her cheek with his thumb.

"Never worked anywhere long enough, too young to draw social security. It'll be a tight couple of years until he turns sixty-five, but he needs to be in assisted living or I'll have a repeat of what happened last week."

He stroked her hair and they lay next to each other in companionable silence.

"So," it was his turn to get flayed open, "I told you mine, tell me yours."

His hand paused mid-stroke and he frowned. "What do you mean? You know my story."

"Does *anyone* know the story of what happened between you and Cash?"

Wincing, he rolled onto his back, keeping her tucked into his side. "I should've known you'd target that, Doc."

"It's not just my job, I do care about you." A lot. Way more than was safe for her heart.

"I told you we were like twins. He was always the wild one and I was always along for the ride." He twined his fingers into hers. "I was the one that wanted to join the Army. Cash is always searching for an adventure—that's why he's the rancher. Working the same field for an entire day, only him and the tractor, he'd be insane in a week. He was always an irresponsible idiot, but it didn't bother me until we deployed."

"How were you two stationed together?"

Dillon blew out a gusty breath. "Freak occurrence during our second enlistment; we ended up in the same platoon, too. I reupped—reenlisted—for another four years because he was going to. I couldn't cut him loose; I functioned as his conscience his whole life. I managed to keep him out of trouble."

He stayed silent so long, she feared he wouldn't continue. His body was rock-hard with tension, nearly vibrating.

"Then…the last deployment. We were clearing a building. I gave him an order to get out of there and he blew me off. He wouldn't have done that with another soldier, but it was me. One of our buddies, Daniels, got killed. He continued sweeping a room and tripped an IED." Dillon swallowed hard. "He was with us one second, gone the next. It happened so fast, pure chaos. Then training kicked in."

He'd hadn't relaxed. His unseeing gaze on the ceiling, likely seeing it all over again.

Elle suspected a story like his, and it explained the lack of pictures. Constant reminders since Cash was probably in most of them. She rested her hand on his chest. His heart beat was quicker than she'd expect for a man lying down. "You felt it was Cash's fault?"

Dillon clenched his jaw. "Yep, he outranked Daniels, should've gotten them both out of that building on my order. But he spun the truth so his ass wouldn't get punished. Daniels took the fall, even after death."

She could ask if he talked to Cash about it, but the answer lay in the silver cans in his fridge. "Then you had to come home and find out your dad was sick, and you missed all that time with him. And, may I add, you felt guilty that you were relieved Cash was all right when another man was killed."

His chest rose under her hand, then fell slowly. He stared at the ceiling, so still. Finally, he blew out a hard breath. "You're good."

She sat up to rearrange the blankets over them. He'd talked and it was more than she'd expected and it was the beginning of what he needed. Maybe now he could sleep the rest of the night without nightmares. And if he had bad dreams, she knew to give him a lot of space.

They couldn't know what the future held, if she could continue seeing him, but tonight, she only needed to snuggle in his arms and sleep in his bed. She needed the comfort as much as he did.

CHAPTER 14

*D*illon stood at the end of his driveway, staring down the road.

Elle clomped up behind him in her boots up the drive. He hadn't been sure she'd woken up when he left the bed. "You could've stayed in bed."

"I couldn't go back to sleep."

He wrapped an arm around her, rubbing her firm ass. "I'll have to make sure I wear you out more." Since she didn't argue, he took it as an open invitation. "Your car will never make it through that."

Her gaze followed his. Several inches of snow had melted the day before, but several inches remained on the roadway. By the end of the weekend, it'd all be melted, but not so she could get home today. The only positive to his pickup getting stolen and being stranded at his house. Elle was stuck with him. No four-wheel drive to give her a ride back to town.

"Are you sure?" She stood on her tiptoes, like it would help her see an extra mile down the road. "The plows haven't come yet?"

"We're not an emergency route. They'll probably be out here later today."

"I'd better go call work." She turned to trudge through his mucky driveway to head back to the house, a frown on her face.

A day of missed clients probably meant a day's less pay for her. She'd mentioned her debt, and with her dad in the nursing home, she was footing that bill, too.

He quickly covered the distance between them. "I can see if Brock can give you a ride to town."

She paused to think about it. "No. He'd have to wait while I got ready at home and then give me a ride to the office. And I'd still be stuck with no vehicle."

"Much of town might still be closed up, digging themselves out. But hey, I threw some of Mama's frozen cinnamon rolls in the oven for breakfast."

The promise of decent food lightened her step as they headed back to the house. He ate with her and headed out to the shop after she offered to clean up.

Figuring she'd just watch a movie or something afterward, he was surprised when the side entrance door opened and Elle strolled in. She wore another sweatshirt and shorts of his and her boots.

"Aren't you cold?" His mind wandered—bra and underwear, or had she gone without?

Shrugging, she wandered around and studied all the equipment. "A little. I thought it might be warmer in here."

"There's no wind in here, but no sunshine, either."

"Can I look through these?" Her hands drifted over the drawers to his chest tool box.

He set the busted scoop bucket tooth down. It'd get welded back on, but not when he could spend time with Elle. "Want to see the place?"

"I don't want to bother you."

"You're never a bother." Taking her hand, he led her to the tractor he hauled snow with. "You saw the big beast that got vandalized. We plow with that one. That's why the tractor's so large, we need a lot of power. This one," he patted the hood of the one they stood next to, "is the workhorse of the yard. Sitting next to it is the attachment to do the majority of the lawn mowing."

"I suppose you don't push mow this much acreage?"

He grinned. "Oh we do that, too. I don't want to scrape this baby against the house's siding, and it doesn't get between the trees well." He continued around, pointing out the various attachments for the yard tractor. "We can also rake ditches with it." At her blank expression, he elaborated. "Mow down a ditch, then rake the clippings into windrows to dry out before bailing."

Elle scrunched her nose at all the equipment. "It's like a whole new language."

"A boring language?"

"I don't think anything you do is boring."

"Then I won't tell you about the seventh day in a row I'm by myself in a tractor cab. Thank God for podcasts." Gesturing to the medium-sized red tractor, he continued. "That one doesn't get used as much, but this is her season. Travis is storing bags of seed that we'll load 'er up with for planting. Travis has a similar model he and Aaron use to plant and haul bales with."

"You don't have anything that's a one job wonder?"

"Some guys get all the newest models, swear by all the gadgets, but our parents were savvy. The least amount of equipment to do the most work, and use it until it dies or it's more expensive to keep running. We can't control the weather, so we need to work smart in every other aspect."

"Where's all the other farming equipment? I at least know what a combine looks like and I don't see one."

"My shop is the only thing I have that's too small." He winked and won a blush. "Aaron and Travis have more acreage to house grain bins and multiple shops for the combines. My patch of land was a tiny, old farmstead before Gramps got a hold of it. The farmhouse was torn down when my dad decided to move out there."

"Too expensive to keep it going?"

His brows drew together. "Good question. Probably fell into disrepair and became a money pit. I guess Gram encouraged them to tear it down. That's all, little lady," he said in his best John Wayne impersonation.

Shivering and hugging her arms around herself, she looked around. "I guess I'd better get inside. Unless," she gave him a saucy look that made his manhood come to attention, "I can bother you with one more thing."

"Any. Time."

Stepping out of her boots, she dropped the shorts and stepped out of them, too. He lifted her against the bench before her feet got cold and dirty. Holding her steady, he wrestled with unzipping his coveralls, but she pitched in and they quickly freed him enough to impale her.

And Dillon got yet another taste of how good having Elle around could be.

THE PLOWS HAD RUMBLED down the road while they'd been eating dinner, but Dillon had recommended letting them dry first. She'd waited until midafternoon before broaching the topic of her leaving.

"You call when you get home." Dillon pressed her against her car and stole a kiss.

"I promise."

Dressed back in her work clothes from Wednesday, she

was ready to brave the mucky road and head back to town. Her first stop would be to check on her dad, but she needed to extract herself from Dillon first.

She needed to *want* to extract herself from him. She'd had more sex in the last three days than the last couple of years combined. Anytime she wanted, he was ready. Anytime he gave her that look, the one with the hooded eyes and suggestive tilt to his full mouth, her clothes peeled themselves off.

She gave him one last nip on his lower lip and opened her door. "Good-bye, Dillon."

"Call me, Elle." He said it like he worried she was driving out of his life.

He wasn't the only one.

She drove away with him standing in her rearview mirror.

The roads were as bad as he'd said. She used all of Dillon's tips for driving on sloppy gravel. Twice, the mud almost won, pulling her car into the pile of snow on the side of the road. But she let off the gas for a second and resisted pulling the wheel sharply in the other direction.

The sound it made when she turned onto the highway was like dozens of tennis balls hitting the body of her car. In both side mirrors, clumps of mud flew off the tires all over the road. Her car must weigh at least two hundred more pounds with all the grit caked on it. The gas station on the edge of town was open twenty-four hours; she'd stop for a quick wash.

The spray took off at least a hundred pounds, but her car still left thick tracks pulling away from the gas station. It would have to do; she needed to check on her dad. She had missed a call from the nursing home while washing her car.

When she reached the nursing home, she stopped at the office before going to her dad's room.

"Hey, Elle. Sorry to bother you." The charge nurse beckoned her in to speak in private. "We just wanted to give you a head's up that the doctor cut down your dad's pain meds and he's not happy about it."

Blood drained from Elle's face. The reality she'd been escaping from for the past three days crashed back into her life.

Once an addict, always an addict.

"He was abusing them." It was a statement not a question.

Wanda nodded. "Given his history and how well he's recovered from the surgery..." She spread her hands. "He was past the point of requiring them, especially at the dose he insisted on."

"I understand. Thanks for letting me know." Woodenly, she walked to her dad's room, dreading the tirade of how unfair everything was, and how unreasonable people could be, and how he was a damn adult.

"Elle." Her dad's greeting was pleasant enough. It always was. "Did Battle-axe Wanda call?"

And it started.

ELLE PARKED at the end of her driveway and groaned. Thank you friendly neighbors for not doing a damn thing. She didn't want to be dependent on other people, but a nice gesture would have been welcome after the conversation with her dad.

Wrestling on her boots, she hit the button to open her garage door and climbed out. Trudging through the mess, she was glad much of it had melted, but now that it was evening, the temperature was dropping. The snow was getting hard and crunchy, requiring extra muscle to hack through it and push it off the concrete. Work that should've invigorated her only dragged her further under a haggard daze.

Working up a sweat, she unzipped her jacket. From the way her shirt stuck to her stomach, she'd need a shower. A warm bath might be more in line with the mental place she loitered in.

She called the driveway good enough after an hour and trudged inside. While running the water in the tub, her phone rang. She contemplated ignoring it, dreading it was the nursing home again and her father was pissed he wasn't getting his narcotics. Always so responsible.

The screen showed it was Dillon.

She shut the water off and stared at it. Part of her wanted desperately to hear his voice, wished he had a vehicle so he could rush over and pleasure the anxiety out of her. The other part didn't want to deal with the dilemma the farm boy presented. He hadn't drunk any alcohol around her, but what if he did? What then? Could she walk after their time together? Probably not if he had a beer, maybe two. If he over imbibed she would be stuck with a major decision.

Her phone went silent. Then started up again. He must be getting worried. She answered.

"Did everything go okay?"

No. And he sounded too good to her ears and frazzled nerves. "Yeah, I just had to shovel out before I could get into the house."

"No one did it for you?" His tone was indignant.

"Nope, the whole block was cleared but my house. 'S okay. I got it."

"It's not okay. I should've called in a favor."

And announce to the community that they were a thing? She wasn't ready. "It's fine. I was just going to take a bath. Talk to you later?" Did that sound like a brush off?

From his silence, yes, it did.

"When can I see you again, Elle?"

She didn't mean to not say anything, but she didn't have an answer. The time with her dad reconstructed the dam around her emotions, stirred all the doubts she'd temporarily shelved. She knew the road her dad's behavior led to, had spent another evening humoring his blubbering over his perceived unfair treatment.

She'd experienced it all before, didn't want to again, but had mentally prepared for the possibility with her dad. Doing any of this with Dillon was out of the question. She'd promised herself not to allow any addiction into her private life beyond what her dad presented her with.

"Tell you what," he filled in, sounding falsely chipper. "Once I get a new pick-up, I'll take you on a date, nice and proper."

She chose an answer that would put off her Dillon dilemma and allow her to sink into her bath and forget the world. "Sure."

"You'll be the first one allowed into my new ride."

She couldn't fight her grin. Giddiness floated through her at the teenage idea she'd get exclusive access to the hot farm boy's new wheels. "Deal."

When he disconnected, she put her phone on vibrate and tossed it into the hallway so nothing would lure her out of bubbly heaven. With a sigh, she sunk into her bath, missing Dillon terribly, and scared that'd be the story of her life.

CHAPTER 15

"So, we heading to the Ford dealership?"

Dillon scowled at Brock as he drove into town. "Fuck you. You know I like quality."

Buying a new truck took his mind off his last conversation with Elle and the growing distance between them that had nothing to do with mileage. It was Monday and he hadn't talked to her since he'd called her Friday after she'd gotten home.

"You like showmanship."

Dillon snorted in disagreement. "I like not having to Fix-Or-Repair-Daily."

They continued their Chevy versus Ford argument all the way to the Chevy dealership. His crashed truck had made the news, but his name had been omitted.

"Hey Dillon, thought I might be seeing you." Sam Johnson swaggered over to them. "Sorry to hear about what happened."

Ah, small town living.

"Thanks, Sam."

All the dealerships thought the Walkers farmed money

trees and people like Sam sought to make a buck off them. Dillon's dad had always said, *You can't save what you spend.*

Sam followed him around the car lot while he looked at the pickups in stock. With every pickup, he got the full rundown and history. Of course, Sam tried to steer him to the brand-spanking new black beauty with all the latest bells and whistles, including the fancy wheel wells that flared out. If Dillon was seventeen, he'd be all over a truck that screamed, *Look at me, I got a truck the size of my balls!* The fifty-five-grand price tag that would drop a good twenty thousand once he drove it off the lot was a big no-deal.

Moore was a small town, but big enough to have a decent variety of vehicles and never a shortage of trucks because it was inhabited by farmers and ranchers. Each dealership made sure to get in a good selection of new and used trucks, but no way in hell was Farmer A going to buy the castoffs of Farmer B. It was just how it worked.

"Tell me about the used red one here." Dillon had looked up the Blue Book value of his destroyed vehicle and calculated how much insurance payout he should get. Going into debt over a perfectly good truck some asshole had destroyed was something Dillon was unwilling to do.

Using funds to buy a flashy vehicle was irresponsible and that was Cash's area.

"Well that one's a couple of years old," Sam said, like it was a bad thing.

In Dillon's mind, it meant it knocked a few thousand off the price and probably came with some extra features. Sam rattled off the details and Dillon worked numbers in his head. To get the same quality pickup and keep from spending thousands of dollars—and answering to Aaron—he'd have to talk Sam down quite a bit on the price.

"I want to try out this one, the used blue one on the end, and the black one next to it."

"You got it, Dillon. I'll be right back." Sam scurried off to grab the keys.

"Coming with?" Dillon asked Brock. He'd promised Elle she'd get the first ride, but technically, he hadn't bought it yet.

"Might as well if I'm going to be fixing it," Brock grumbled, but he didn't mind. The dude in both of them always liked driving new vehicles. Sam came out and tossed them the keys for the red one. "Grab me when you get back and I'll get you set up in the blue one."

Dillon took the standard route for test driving. He drove through town, hit some dirt roads, and took it out on the highway. The exact same route his dad had taken with every vehicle he'd ever purchased. He was pretty sure this was the one he'd go with, but wasn't impulsive enough to buy it without trying a couple of others first. Another dad lesson.

"Elle get home okay?" Brock asked.

Dillon couldn't avoid the topic with his cousins forever. They all pressed into his personal business, but he never indulged much. He watched out for them, not the other way around.

"I wish you hadn't dragged her into it." But then Elle wouldn't have been his for days.

A hint of memory of what went on between them threatened to make him hard. Bad timing.

"You know I had to," Brock grumbled. "We couldn't be saddled with that liability."

"Well, she got home okay."

"When?"

Dillon aimed the pickup to head back to town. "Friday."

Brock gave him the side-eye and whistled. "Nice. She's cute."

She's sexy as hell. "Yeah."

"Something going on between you two?"

It was tempting to say no, keep Elle his little secret in case she cut and run, but he found himself saying, "Trying like hell."

Brock smirked. "Good. You gotta work for it."

"Since when have *you* ever had to work for it?" Brock might be more concerned about what's under the hood of a GTO than between a girl's legs, but that didn't stop girls from flocking to him.

"Finding love for more than one night isn't easy. No one wants forever with a gearhead."

Dillon glanced at his cousin. In no way would he have thought Brock nursed a lonely heart. Again, the sense of distance between him and his cousins nagged him. In high school, they'd always approached him for advice. Nowadays, not so much.

"The right one's out there for you. You might have to convince her like I need to do with Elle."

"That serious, huh?"

"On my end, yes. On hers? I'm working on it."

"Women," Brock snorted.

"Exactly."

They test drove the other two trucks but Dillon's intuition had been right. The red one was the best deal and drove real nice. With the paperwork done, he wrote a check. It hurt, writing one for that much but once the insurance money came in he could pay three-quarters of it back. If they ever found out who wrecked his other truck, he'd make sure he got the rest. Legally, of course.

After Dillon was handed the keys, Brock left, muttering about being behind on his work. Dillon drove his new ride straight to the nursing home to visit Gram.

"There's my lady," he greeted, strolling in.

"Oh, Dillon, what a surprise."

"Sorry I couldn't make it yesterday."

Her shrewd gaze pinned him. "Well, when you don't have a set of wheels, it's hard to get to town."

Ducking his head, he grinned at her. "Heard about that, didya?"

Gram chuckled. "A nursing home concentrates the gossip of a small town. Which means, I also heard of the vandalism."

Dillon met her weary blue gaze. "Sorry I didn't tell you at first Gram. I just didn't want to worry you and we didn't have much information."

"Tsk, tsk, Dillon. Shouldering the weight of the world again. It gets pretty heavy." She sighed and leaned back in her rocking chair. "I'm old, but I'm a farm wife. I can take a lot."

Gram was the toughest woman he'd ever met, outmatching all of the hard-asses in the Army he'd come across.

"We don't know who's behind it, or why."

She aimed a thousand yard stare out the window. "History likes to repeat itself."

"What do you mean?"

Gram snapped her gaze toward him. "People always messing with stuff that's not theirs. Never changes no matter what year it is."

Dillon narrowed his eyes at her. Either she was smoothly steering the conversation where she wanted it, like Sam the salesman, or she was losing her mind. Each week, she said something that just wasn't his sharp-minded Gram.

"Since you're here now, you must have a new pickup. Tell me about it."

He'd keep an eye on her, maybe ask the others if they experienced anything similar.

∾

SINCE HIS TIME with Elle revealed how pathetic his food supply was, Dillon pushed a wobbly cart through Better Grocers. He was a grown man and shouldn't be living off his mama's cooking. She was a damn good cook, though. He also suspected that as long as his future wife didn't mind, his mama would continue to supply them with a month's worth of food.

Future wife.

Was it too early to get that serious about Elle? Because he totally could. She was more than he'd ever found in a woman. Intelligent, driven, sweet, and tenacious in bed.

His shop, against his workbench. Groaning, he buried the thought in the recesses of his mind until he was home, in the shower.

Turning down the cereal aisle, he almost ran into another cart. He looked up to apologize and found himself staring into a beautiful pair of surprised green eyes.

"Hey," he smiled. He'd get groceries more often if he could run into Elle each time.

"Dillon!" She backed her cart up and he pulled his beside hers. She peeked inside. "Replenishing?'

"Is it replenishing if there was nothing there in the first place?" He gave her cart a once over, noting leafy greens, red apples, and bananas. "Looks like I forgot a whole department.

"It's called produce and it's at the end of the store. You should check it out sometime," she teased.

"I'd do that if I had someone who knew their way around it. Know anyone?"

She chuckled. "What are you doing in town? Did you get a new vehicle?"

"Purdy little red thing sitting out in the lot." He seized the opportunity. "I'm starving. Let's pick something up to eat at your place and then I'll take you for a spin."

Good thing he wasn't a betting man, because if he'd wagered that she'd say yes, he'd be awfully worried about losing all his money. She was chewing on her bottom lip, her gaze avoiding his, eyeing her groceries instead.

"We can call it that date you promised me," he urged.

Elle relaxed a little, the idea actually seemed to please her. "Can you assemble ingredients, or do we need to buy it fully prepared to throw in an oven?"

"I made a perfectly fine grilled cheese, if I do remember."

The way she beamed up at him through her lashes…he could get used to seeing that for forever.

"How about spaghetti?" she offered.

"Let's get shopping."

A TASK as mundane as grocery shopping transformed into a fun event with Dillon, once she left her self-consciousness in the cereal aisle.

He cracked jokes all the way through the store and stopped to chat with every old farmer they crossed. It was like they all belonged to a secret club, spoke their own language, their grimy trucker hats serving as an ID badge.

She stuffed down the worry that she and Dillon would be the talk of the town. Worst case scenario: the old farmers would peg her as the new counselor. She had her own cart, filled with her own groceries, and was meandering through the place next to Dillon. Maybe they'd think they were seeing each other, maybe not. Elle couldn't let the what-ifs run—or ruin—her night.

He followed her home and swore his groceries would be fine in the bed of his truck since the evenings this time of year dropped to much cooler temps. "Mobile refrigeration."

Over dinner, she'd asked him why he was in town so late.

"Grandma Agnes. I missed my Sunday showing and had to make it up."

"Had to?"

"Can't miss a week with Grandma. Just ain't right. Today was a nice treat. The fields need more drying time, giving me a day to just run errands."

Twirling her spaghetti onto her fork, wistful thoughts filled her head. She'd love to be excited about visiting her dad. Instead it was a duty, the parent/child roles had reversed years earlier. His attitude toward a decline in pain meds taxed her tolerance, so she'd taken a couple of days off from visiting him, making a quick check-in call once a day.

He tapped her nose.

She jerked back. "What was that for?"

"You were getting lost in that pretty little head of yours."

He seemed to know when she'd retreated into her anxiety. The night was such a lovely change of plans from doing nothing that she didn't want to dive into her latest daddy issues.

"Wanna ride before the sun sets?" he asked with a boyish grin.

A smile of relief curved her mouth. "Sounds divine."

He grabbed her hand and pulled her outside.

When she stepped into the pickup, he assisted her with a hand on her waist.

She'd missed him. Her body missed him, her eyes couldn't soak him in enough. Two days had felt like two weeks.

Tomorrow she planned to remedy her quiet evenings by taking the advice she'd dished out to many clients. Being settled into her house and job, her dad nestled in the nursing home, opened up time for much needed workouts.

But this was so much better.

His new pickup was more than nice. While it had to cost three times more than any car she'd ever bought, which was two total, it wasn't the newest thing on the market. Her time at his farm taught her that their possessions might be quality, but they were functional and well cared for, like the equipment in his shop. The red pickup probably transformed like Optimus Prime into some other farm equipment. Examining the spacious cab, she thought it could double as an RV.

"Do you fish?"

She'd been so lost in thought, she wondered if she'd missed an entire hunk of conversation. "Nooo?"

"You grew up in the land of ten thousand lakes, but never went fishing?"

"I still grew up a city girl, fishing was not on my radar. Ironic, since I spent so much time in the water."

"Tonight, you get the tour of the main fishing area for Moore, but when the roads clear up, I'll show you the Walkers' private fishing hole."

Her interest perked up at the mention of a body of water on their property. "Do you only fish there or can you swim at all?"

"Oh, there's been plenty of times the boys, and rumor has it, Cash's little sister, have been in that water, but I don't think swimming was their intention." At her raised eyebrow, he explained with a wicked grin. "They'd take their dates there, you know, for a swim with no clothes."

Laughing with Dillon never grew old. "I can't say we never had those stories on the swim decks, but I think that's all they were. I'm not so sure with your family."

"Do you miss it?"

"Yes. I worked so hard on the swim team, and then my degree was done and I haven't stepped into a pool since." The idea of swimming laps for an hour equated ultimate boredom to many, but swimming was meditation for Elle. "Does Moore even have an indoor pool?"

"Other than the two hotels in town that have small ones?

Not yet, but last year the town voted in a new family gym facility."

"When are they going to build the place?" Resting her head back, watching scenery go by, she made a mental note to check on the details. Like how much a membership cost.

"I think they broke ground already. I didn't pay much attention cuz I wasn't seeing a sexy swimmer at the time. You probably hadn't moved here yet when the excitement was swirling around town." He turned onto a small two-lane highway. "Lake Osborne is the largest lake in the county. This highway goes right through it, so there's shore fishin' and a boat ramp off both sides."

Four miles later, he pulled into one of the lots around the boating ramp.

"I'm surprised it's empty. But I guess it's getting late, and it's a Monday night." Swinging around like he was going to drive out, he stopped and threw the truck in park. "Want to get out and walk around? Get up an up-close view of Lake Osborne? We missed the sunset, but I can leave the head-lights on for us."

Smiling, she shook her head. "Maybe another time. I'm just kind of comfortable here, enjoying learning about my new home.'

He draped an arm on the wheel, the other resting across the seatback. He looked good sitting like that. His worn base-ball cap lent him bad boy charm, and the twist in his torso stretched his shirt over his chest. Since his jacket hung open, she ogled all she wanted. Because she knew what that chest looked like naked.

"How comfortable are you Elle?" His voice dropped a suggestive octave.

Not comfortable enough. The stirring of desire she'd been holding at a sane limit roared right past those barriers. She'd expected to go home, have a solitary dinner, and read until bed. But here sat a sexual god that could turn her legs to jelly and make her voice raw from passion.

"Shut off the headlights." She sat forward to take her jacket off.

"Yes, ma'am." He shut everything off and killed the engine.

The console was raised to its upright position. He leaned over, closing the space between them, his face close, lips hovering just above hers. Reaching to the other side of the seat, he pulled a lever and her seat tipped back.

She yelped. He chuckled, following her down to capture her lips.

God it felt good to kiss him again, to have his weight settled on top of her. Except…

"Dillon," she managed to get out while he was kissing her senseless. He waited, his lids heavy. "I don't want to, you know, undress all the way, in case…" Getting busted naked at Lake Osborne wasn't on her grown professional woman bucket list.

"I got an idea," he said licking the seam of her lips. "Undo your pants." She complied, he unbuttoned his. Caressing the side of her face, he murmured, "Roll over."

She turned, figuring out the logistics as she went, her insides going wild at his plan. The lot they were parked in sat lower than the highway, but there'd be enough light from the moon, not to mention any approaching car's headlights, that they could see what was going on inside.

She was willing to risk it; she needed him inside her.

He maneuvered behind her, and yanked her pants down. His erection strained out of his zipper, rubbing between her ass cheeks. He reached around to ready her, his fingers hitting the mark immediately. The thought of being with Dillon had already dampened her panties.

She groaned and pushed back into him. He stroked her

for only a moment before freeing himself to push in. She couldn't spread her legs like she wanted, her face was shoved into the seat back, but none of it mattered when he seated himself inside. He pumped, she held on, afraid she'd put claw marks in his new ride.

"I'm not going to last long, Elle," he whispered harshly in her ear. She shivered against him and raised her head. "You're so fucking wet, I can't slow down."

Headlights appeared in the distance. Her eyes widened, he followed her gaze and increased the pressure with his fingers.

"Come for me, Elle."

Absolutely. He surrounded her; his breath at her neck, his fingers at her sex, thrusting into her from behind. The headlights and their voyeuristic effect had her grabbing the seat sides and slamming back into him.

He worked her ruthlessly until she shook underneath him, swearing her heart would give out or her climax would last until the car was close enough to witness her finish. With a grunt, and three more slams into her, he hugged her tight and moaned into her neck.

There was no time to bask in the afterglow. Dillon rolled off her and helped adjust her clothing, before settling his back into place. Both of them stilled, watching the headlights come closer. Would the car keep going, or turn off to check on them?

Elle sagged in relief when the car passed. Dillon stared at her with a bemused expression.

"Can I help you?" she asked archly.

Slowly, he grinned. "Oh, honey, you already have."

Thankfully it was dark and he couldn't see her blush. Sex in a vehicle was marked off her list and she hadn't known it'd been added. With Dillon, sex was always off the charts, so powerful it clouded her thinking.

That was a sobering thought. "I'd better get home. I don't want to be short of sleep this early in the week."

His smile died. He fired up the engine and they drove back to town. He pointed out places they passed and filled her in with its history and information, which she acknowledged with one- or two-word answers.

As Dillon walked her to her door like a gentleman, she wasn't sure if he'd ask to come inside, ask to stay the night. She wasn't sure she'd say no, but she had to think about herself and her job.

He gave her a sweet kiss, said he'd call her later, and left.

She went inside and watched him drive off, giving a little wave. Already, she wished she had invited him in.

CHAPTER 16

*D*illon slept too late again. The weather was supposed to cooperate today and the spring sun had dried the fields enough he could get back in them and he'd lost three hours. It'd be a late night to make up for it.

He rolled off the couch. The pile of silver cans on the carpet mocked him. Last night had been a mind-blowing experience with Elle in his truck. She'd wanted him as badly as he'd needed her and they came together explosively, like two horny teenagers who were so addicted to each other they snuck around anytime and anywhere. His mind started imagining what it'd be like to take Elle to the family's fishing hole, pack a lunch and a comfy blanket, and make love under the stars. Or wrap up with her on the back deck. Soon he could pull the grill out and surprise her with a romantic picnic right outside the sliding doors.

His pants hadn't even been zipped shut when she'd closed herself off to him, destroyed the bubbling well of fantasies as soon as they'd started.

Running a hand through his hair and groaning, he

stooped to pick up the cans. The familiar headache and cotton mouth called for a solid breakfast.

Shuffling into the kitchen, he aimed for the fridge. He poured himself some orange juice and turned to consider the bags of groceries resting on his counter. The juice hit the spot and drove off some of the headache. He tackled the unloading, grateful he hadn't been so unsettled from Elle's reaction after sex to forget to put the cold items away.

Kitchen cleaned up, he dressed, packed a lunch for the field, dug out headphones to listen to tunes on his phone, and locked up the house.

The morning had been good up to that point.

Score marks on the door frame and around the knob marred the exterior of the door. He stepped back to appraise his driveway, his stomach sinking and churning at the same time. Tire tracks that weren't from his vehicle decorated the space in front of the shop. There weren't skid marks. Someone one had driven up just to bust into his shop?

He dug his phone out of pocket and called Brock.

His cousin answered. "The tractor acting up again?"

"I haven't made it to the field yet." Admitting his lapse in responsibility stuck in his craw. Brock had probably been up since before sunrise to tinker on his Mustangs. Dillon mentally snorted. Brock probably slept in his 'Stangs.

"What's going on, then? Missed my voice?"

"We've had a visitor again."

"I'll be right over."

Dillon snapped pictures and called Deputy Max—a routine that was becoming all too familiar.

Both men arrived, hugging the edge of the driveway so Max could inspect the tracks and the damage.

Another hour ticked by. He'd be lucky to finish his work before sundown. He might as well pack dinner, too.

Max left after gathering his own pictures and Dillon's statement.

Brock adjusted his Ford racing hat, a nervous tick when he didn't want to say what he was thinking.

"What's going on in that thick head of yours, Brock?"

"I was just wondering why you didn't hear this guy pull up."

Dillon flushed hot under his collar as he scowled. "It's not like they came rolling up with an engine roaring like your Shelby GTO. Modern cars are quiet, his lights were probably off. I can't hear the crunch of gravel from my bed." Or the couch, where he'd actually spent the night.

"What time did ya get home last night?"

"I wasn't at the bar if that's what you're asking. I was out with Elle. Got home and went to bed." After easing his frustrations with the gorgeous counselor by relaxing with a few beers. "I don't need to be interrogated. I'm not the one picking locks."

His cousin took off his cap, ran his hand through his jet-black hair, and set his beloved cap back in place. "I know, man. Keep an eye out. Maybe we should look at getting a security system." Brock hissed in disgust. "It'd cost a fortune to set up five homes."

Dillon had come to the same conclusion. "Better sooner than later. I got a feeling he ain't done with us."

"Yeah. I'll talk to the others while you're working. Aaron is hitting the quarter behind his house and Travis is helping Cash with the cattle."

Dillon clapped Brock on the shoulder and headed in to get the tractor fired up. He ambled outside and maneuvered it in front of the chisel plow attachment to hook on for a day that included lunch and supper in the cab of the tractor and a sore ass. Throwing his cooler and gear into the storage area behind the driver's seat, he stepped down to give everything a once-over before he headed out.

The approach of summer was evident in the warmer winds and longer days. Trees would soon fill with green buds and the lilacs surrounding his place would be in full bloom and even as a dude, he had to admit, shit was pretty. He couldn't wait to show Elle around the farm when the land hit its lush state.

She'd never been fishing, he doubted she'd ever ridden a horse. His summer goals were to remedy that, after conquering her fears about them as a couple.

How she'd grown up created an obstacle. Sneaking around is what he felt like he was doing with Elle. Only Brock knew about them. At best, his other cousins might suspect he was seeing someone. He'd bet all the silver cans lining his fridge that she hadn't told anyone.

She was the best thing to happen to him—ever—but he didn't want to be her dirty little secret. Ashamed of being seen with him wasn't her hang-up. He was a good-looking guy, well respected around town by those who knew him. As for the work issue, rip it off like a Band-Aid. Waltz through town, her hand on his arm, proving they're a good couple and *appropriate*.

He wanted to take her out for dinner, maybe some dancing, but she'd sounded noncommittal to every suggestion. "How about a movie," he'd asked.

"Maybe," she'd replied, "see how the weekend goes."

Again, it went back to her dad. She was afraid he was like her dad, was unwilling to be stuck taking care of everything while he wasted away in his mental illness.

He wasn't an alcoholic and if she spent more time around him, she'd realize that.

Whittling Elle's resistance down became top priority for

him. Business might be heading into the busy season, but he'd never be too busy for Elle.

"It's Mental Health Wednesday," Betsy sang at the door to Elle's office. "I'm not giving up on yo-ou-ou-ou."

Elle grinned and spun to face her friend. "If I say yes, will you quit singing?"

Betsy gasped in false outrage. "I have never had any complaints about my singing—for at least two weeks."

"Same place, same time?"

"Absolutely."

"I'm almost done and I'll meet you there."

Betsy pinned her with her sternest mom look. "I'll believe it when I see it, chickadee."

"I promise," Elle called to Betsy's back as she walked away.

She wrapped up her documentation, grabbed her stuff, and walked briskly to her car. Excitement about the night out with friends bubbled over until she smiled to herself. The lot was almost empty, her car the last one, and an older pickup she'd never seen before parked down the street. A sense of déjà vu swept over her. Only Brock's truck was nicer.

She wouldn't have paid much attention, but compared to what the Walkers drove, the truck looked so…used and abused. Was she developing a nothing-compares-to-a-red-Chevy complex?

Nothing compared to the man who drove one.

Dillon filled her thoughts on her way to the bar and grill. She only thought about him twenty times—a minute. He wanted a date, had asked her officially, and received no real answer from her.

Commitment issues, party of one?

Solid reasons formed her misgivings and one of them sat grumbling in a nursing home a mile away. Elle mentally prepped herself for a weekend of moving him into the assisted living apartment that would be his new home.

Dad will be fine. He had no car, and nurses monitored his meds. He actually appeared excited and her new reality might include more freedom.

Hadn't she thought that before? Then he'd gotten cancer and she couldn't bear to move out on him. Like her, he had no one else.

None of those thoughts tonight, she resolved as she strode into the noisy bar and grill. Betsy whooped and waved for her to join them.

The night went by in a blur of good food, rowdy laughter, and loud music. One by one, her coworkers filtered out, all citing an early morning. Elle should be leaving too, but dang it, she was having fun.

Betsy sat with her for another hour before looking at her watch. "Well, the kids should all be in bed. That means all the work is done and it's safe to head home."

Elle gasped dramatically. "You were just using me?"

"Of course. Why do you think I've been nagging you to come out?" Betsy shrugged on her coat and waited for Elle.

"Go ahead, Betsy. I need to hit the ladies room first."

Betsy went out the front and Elle went in search of the bathroom.

She should've paid more attention exiting the bathroom, but she was straightening her purse strap to sling it over her shoulder and ran smack into another body. Her purse dropped to the floor, keys and lip gloss spilling out.

"Sorry!" She bent down to pick her stuff up.

"It's no problem," a deep voice answered. A large man knelt down in front of her. "It's my fault."

Scarred, tanned hands helped gather her things. Flustered, she tossed them into her bag and straightened.

He stood, his deep brown eyes sweeping her body with open male appreciation. His attention did nothing for her rattled state.

"It was an accident," she said, breathless from the quick squat and grab, which unfortunately sounded flirty.

Avid masculine interest was rare for her. And when she was in emotional turmoil about what to do with Dillon? Her frayed nerves prepared to ward off another six-foot-two male, because one was too many, thank you very much.

Brown eyes twinkled, a slow smile spread across his lips. "It's never the woman's fault. My mama taught me that."

She answered with a quick smile, barely able to hold it with the man's full presence towering over her.

With his swarthy good looks, he wouldn't have trouble casting a net for lonely women and reeling it in plum full. His use of "mama" made her think of Dillon, like everything else did. Guilt rose, as if being in a bar, getting hit on by a hot guy put her on the wrong side of right with Dillon.

"Your mom was right. It's good of you to remember. Thank you for helping me pick my things up." She pivoted to move around him.

"Are you from here?" He sidestepped in front of her. "It's just that I'm new to town, don't know many people." He stuck out his hand. "Jesse Rodriguez."

No way to extract herself without being rude. "Elle. And no, I'm not native to Moore."

He shook her hand like a caress, and pre-Dillon Walker, she would've been open to his flirtation.

"How long have you lived here?" Slowly he released her

hand, his eyes never leaving hers in a way that made her feel like the only woman in the place.

"I moved in the last year." She was never too specific with strangers, especially men. Pointing in the direction of the parking lot before he could ask any more questions, she said, "I need to get going. Nice to meet you, Jesse."

"Nice to run into you. It's a small town, maybe see you around?"

She didn't know what to say that wouldn't invite unwanted attention, so she left with a small nod and wove through the throng of people. A month ago, running into Jesse would have been a welcome occurrence, now...Dillon Walker.

Driving out of the parking lot, she saw the same beat up truck that was parked near her workplace.

Huh. It really was a small town.

CHAPTER 17

"Movie night tomorrow night?" Dillon asked Elle hopefully, the phone with shitty reception pressed to his ear.

He was perched in the cab of the tractor. His dinner, a cold sandwich, rested on his knee, but he couldn't wait any longer. By the time he got home, she'd probably be in bed. He hadn't talked to her since Monday evening. It was Thursday and he got tired of waiting for her to call.

"I went out with some coworkers last night and I think I'm still recovering. Not used to all this socializing."

She'd gone out? While he'd been bumping along, staring at a stretch of black topsoil, planning a date with her. Jealousy wasn't an emotion he was familiar with—normally. And it wasn't envy, but rather resentment because of her resistance to him.

No, he wouldn't go there. Good for her. Her coworkers may be able to loosen her up so she'd realize dating in a small town wasn't the gossip fest she thought. It was Moore. Half her coworkers might have met their spouses through work.

"Movie night in, then? I can come into town after work so you don't have to go anywhere." *And no one has to see us.*

"I don't have cable. Can you bring the movie?"

He'd take every advantage he could. "Absolutely. Are you in the mood for something exciting or something mellow?"

"Mellow, I think. No wait. I have to get up early Saturday and pack the rest of Dad's stuff and move him. I don't want a late night before that."

Her voice weighed heavy with fatigue, whether physical or emotional, he didn't know. He felt like an ass for pushing her. Sleeping twelve hours on a Friday night was probably right up her alley.

"I'll run to town Saturday morning and help you load up."

"Thanks, Dillon, but I rented a moving van."

What the hell for? "Why didn't you call me? I'm begging to be yours to command."

"You're busy Dillon. I didn't want to impose."

"Elle, it's okay to ask for help."

"I moved us to town. I can move dad across the nursing home to the assisted living wing."

He pictured her wrestling the mattresses out of the door and into a moving van. All. By. Herself.

Stubborn woman.

"Elle, go to bed early tomorrow night, get some rest. I'm coming to help you Saturday. Then I'm taking you out. Somewhere nice. I'll be there by nine." That should give her some time to sleep in. She took a breath that sounded like a sigh, probably ready to argue. "I'm down to one bar for reception, I'd better go. See you Saturday."

"Dil—"

He tapped the angry red button on his phone. Or maybe he was the angry one. More like frustrated. On Saturday, he needed to know where he sat with her. Using him for his body would be fine if he didn't want so much more from her.

THE EXCUSE of *I'll burn it all off moving* was enough for Elle to pick out two pints of ice cream. The real stuff. The hold-no-fat-and-calories-back kind that cost double what any other pint did. What else went with a Friday night where she'd turned down the guy that made her toes curl?

While waiting behind two heaping-full shopping carts to check out, a deep, familiar voice said her name.

"Elle, right?"

She spun around, a flare of excitement bubbling up before her brain could register that it wasn't Dillon. Jesse stood holding his own carry-basket full of dude food like cans of beef stew and soda. Wearing grease-marked clothing with a tab that indicated he worked as a mechanic, he still turned a girl's head.

"Hi, Jesse."

"Wild Friday night, eh?" He nodded toward her basket of ice cream and more ice cream. And bananas because she was always responsible.

"You know it. Same goes for you?"

"A guy's gotta eat." He smiled, his gaze unwavering.

The intense scrutiny should be flattering, but years of sitting in a small office with people with mental disorders gave her an acute awareness of when someone was "off." Jesse…she wasn't sure.

The line moved and she shuffled forward.

"A girl's gotta eat, too." He moved with her. "Can I take you out for some real food tomorrow night?"

"Thanks for the offer, Jesse, but I have plans." *Tell him you have a boyfriend!* But the words didn't come. What else was Dillon to her?

"I can get your number so we can plan another time."

"I'm sorry, Jesse. I'm seeing someone." There! She'd said it.

"Ah, thus the plans." His grin was friendly, but his gaze held a touch of coolness. From her rejection? "Can't blame a guy for trying. You're a beautiful woman."

"Well, thank you. Hope you can *run* into another lady who's not taken," she said lightly, referring to how they'd met.

A hint of smugness lit his dark eyes. "Running into stuff isn't my problem." He jutted his chin to the moving line behind her. "You're up, Elle. Don't want you wasting time on me while your ice cream's melting. That's the high-octane stuff, right there."

Nervously laughing at his comment, she dropped her groceries on the belt and tapped her foot while they were rung up.

She grabbed her bag and shot Jesse a departing smile and received a stiff smile in return.

Her night afterward was uneventful.

The odd interaction had been the first thing on her mind when she woke, but in true Dillon fashion, he soon dominated her thoughts. No point staying in bed; it was the last place safe for daydreaming about Dillon.

She jumped out of bed and gobbled down breakfast. Next up was choosing clothes to haul boxes and furniture in. She threw on a pair of yoga pants and a plain yellow shirt that would pick up every speck of dust but was comfortable and didn't show her ass when she bent down.

Her dad didn't need a lot of possessions, but she'd stripped his bed and cleaned and packed all the bedding earlier in the week. Then she'd finished packing the rest of his clothing that he hadn't needed in the nursing home. Those boxes, along with bins of his knickknacks and books, sat in the garage. She'd cancelled the moving van since Dillon had so graciously demanded to help her move.

Other than the bed and another chair to add to the one

they would move from his current room in the nursing home to his new one in the assisted living wing, her dad had a folding table. She'd find him a real table, a small round one that'd fit better in the small apartment.

With Dillon's help it wouldn't take long. Then she'd be with the farm boy the rest of the day. Her stomach flipped in anticipation.

One last look through her dad's things to make sure she'd gathered everything for him. Her garage was chilly, but not unbearable and she wasn't going to be long. She toed a box. Books. Another box. More books.

Huh. She didn't remember her dad reading so much. Would he want these? Should she buy him new ones? What did he read?

She didn't know what her dad liked to read. Scowling at the boxes, she shoved them over to get at the lighter boxes. In hindsight, she should've wielded a sharpie and done some labeling.

She flipped open the lid on one and froze.

Pictures. Framed pictures, loose pictures, newspaper clippings. Pulling one into the light, she read through the stats and found her name. Third place in the freestyle at regionals her junior year of high school.

Her dad had saved all these? He'd clipped them in the first place?

Perching on a book box, she shuffled through the contents. A framed picture of her and her dad standing in front of a brick wall stumped her. She had no memory of when that had been taken, couldn't guess where. An aquatic center, judging by the background, and she must've been— she squinted at the image of herself--fifteen. She'd been fifteen.

She didn't remember it at all, but her dad had gone as far as developing and framing the photo.

She stuffed everything back inside, save the swimming photo, and moved onto the next box.

Swim medals.

Next box. She flipped the lid and slammed it shut again. A brief glimpse of her mother's face left her heart racing.

With extreme care, she peeled back the cardboard flap and stared at the happy family. The photo had been taken during a weekend of camping, and there in the campsite was a liter of cola and a glass bottle of whiskey.

The couple who drinks together certainly didn't stay together.

She frowned as memories churned. Her mom sleeping on the couch with an empty bottle on the end table. An adult's recollection of her childhood interpreted data differently.

Another forgotten memory. Her mom used to drink as much as her dad. Did she still?

Elle shook her head. She'd never know and she didn't want to know.

The doorbell rang. Everything was closed up and pushed back in place.

She trotted inside, dropping the picture into a box to bring to her dad's new place. Her discovery was dismissed as anticipation of seeing Dillon took over. She opened the front door to see him reclined against the railing, arms folded, cap pulled down. His gaze wary about the reception he'd get. Was a man who looked that good ever received badly?

"Hi," she greeted. "Come in."

He stepped in close to her. She made the first move, rising up to her toes to give him a kiss.

His arms snaked around her and he immediately deepened the kiss. How easily she could blow off the whole day and spend it naked with him.

Finally, he pulled away. "That's a better welcome than I thought I'd get."

"You *were* a little bossy."

Blue eyes twinkled down at her. "I'm starting to wonder if that's how I need to be."

"Don't push it."

Laughing, he looked around. "Tell me what to move. I am at your service." He winked. "*All* day."

Oh, she'd get to that. "Furniture first while we're fresh, then boxes."

"Yes, ma'am."

CHAPTER 18

They'd just brought the last of the boxes when Elle's dad showed up.

Dillon set his box down in the corner and shook Gary's hand. Elle's dad was a few inches shorter than him. Perhaps before the man's health declined, he'd been more robust.

Gary continued into the room, shuffling his walker in front of him. "Thank you for helping Elle. She's so stubborn, I feared she'd try to do everything herself."

Dillon arched an eyebrow at Elle. "I know what you mean."

"Everything's moved Dad," Elle said, ignoring him. "We'll run and stock you up on some groceries. Do you just want a sandwich for dinner?"

"Oh, I thought you two might join me for—" Gary paused, eyeing the both of them. "A sandwich would be great. Don't forget the chips."

"Of course."

Dillon followed her out. He hated missing the opportunity to get to know her dad, but dinner with Gary wasn't a real date with Elle.

Groceries were purchased in record time. Elle was quick and efficient, knowing exactly what her dad liked and didn't like, and what he could have and not have. They unloaded and left with Elle promising Gary she'd pick up more food before she visited next.

"Can I use your place to get cleaned up?" he asked as they were walking out for the last time that day.

"Sure. I need to shower, too."

Thoughts of her in the shower, water sluicing off her satiny skin…they hadn't done anything in the shower yet.

He intended to remedy that.

And he did, ten minutes after she'd entered the shower. He'd asked if she needed help reaching her back.

She'd invited him in.

Shower sex had been mind blowing. The chemistry, the connection between them, had heightened every sensation. The only reason he hadn't carried her to bed and remained there all weekend was because he wanted his date.

"Have you been to the Crazy Eights Tavern yet?" he called from the living room.

"No," she replied from her bedroom, where she was still getting ready.

When she'd asked what to wear, he'd said dancing clothes. When she hadn't quit staring at him, he'd been concerned he needed alternate plans.

"What kind of dancing?" she'd asked.

Like there was more than one? "Country."

It had been enough of an answer for her. She'd disappeared into her room for twenty minutes.

As she emerged, he swallowed his tongue. Good god, the woman had legs. Toned and long, they made her skinny jeans look good, not the other way around. A gauzy, deep green belted shirt accented her hips and bust, while her boots made his mouth water.

Boots like that were country boy kryptonite. Fancier than work boots, they had buckles that teased the imagination and rose all the way to her knees. He liked a challenge.

Her hair hung loose, curtaining her face, adding a healthy dose of sexy on top of her knockout outfit.

"Damn," was all he could say.

She flashed him a small smile. "Thank you. I'm starving."

Food wasn't on his mind. Not enough blood remained in his head to think. He held an arm out, she snaked hers through, and he led her out to his farmer's chariot.

Striding through the tavern, he nodded at people he knew, keeping Elle tucked in close. Interest percolated in those who acknowledged him in return because he hadn't been seen with a girl on a real date since before leaving for basic training. Elle was new to town and didn't go out much. She was an enigma, and she was his.

Once they were settled into a booth, he watched her peruse the menu. "What are you having?"

"Grilled shrimp. I can never cook it the way restaurants do. It doesn't stop me from trying, but I love to eat the good stuff when I can." She looked up, saw his menu closed on the table. "Let me guess. Steak?"

"Ding, ding, ding."

"Isn't that akin to heresy, ordering a steak that's not from your ranch?"

"Ordering a turkey burger would be wrong. Ordering steak is never wrong."

Her laughter chimed its way through him. It was good to be with her. Not just when naked, but hanging out. Talking.

After they ordered, she twirled her straw in her ice water. He had ordered water out of respect for her. When their relationship grew, and she trusted him, he'd have a beer now and then.

Pushing her water to the side, she settled back. "So what's

farm life like? I learned a little since I've known you, but what's the daily grind?"

Was there a simple answer for it? "Like military life in a way. Hurry up and wait. Long stretches of boring work with sudden bouts of excitement, not always the good kind. In the Army, we had to perform common task training every year. Farming is similar. It isn't step one, do this, step two…like Army training, but I have machinery to maintain, equipment maintenance, manuals to refresh my memory on."

"I'd have never equated the two."

"Me, either," he laughed. "My military buddies thought farming was in my blood or something. It is, absolutely, but there's a lot of science. Economics if you don't want to go bust. And the planning. Me and the guys meet once a month, have a real meeting."

"Really?"

"We rent a meeting room, order lunch, bring our records and updates, so it feels all official."

"I thought you guys were always in contact."

"We are." He snagged her hand, studying her fingers while he talked. "One at a time. Maybe a couple of us will hang out, but getting all five of us together takes planning. Organizing a meeting increases the likelihood it won't get blown off because when we're in our own space, we get distracted with repairs and chit-chat and whatever else comes up. We've got to make it feel legit. Then lunch is tax deductible."

She smiled, her gaze dropping to their intertwined hands. "How do you decide when to do stuff, like plowing and planting and harvesting?"

"Plowing, if needed, in the spring when the snow melts and the ground thaws. Discing used to be done after to smooth it out for planting, which we'd do about the middle of May. But that's old-school thinking. Most years, we don't even need to plow. The stuff left over after harvest is good food and breaks down better without being plowed. Sometimes I still do it, it all depends. The summer is filled with haying, treating, and irrigating until harvest. Harvest is its own beast, but we're already planning seed for the next planting season."

"What do you during the winter?"

He leaned back so the server could set their plates down. "Everything else. After harvest, I help Cash work cattle, move them to winter pasture, stack hay. Equipment maintenance. You saw how we dealt with snow."

"That was a lot of snow." She dug into her food.

Dillon had schemed to get her talking before she asked him more questions. He didn't mind discussing his life, but she used it to evade discussing hers. "Your turn."

"I already told you." She went from chowing shrimp to pushing rice around her plate.

"You gave me the Cliffs Notes. I want to hear about *you*."

She stalled with a drink of water before she settled back. "What do you want to know?"

"What was growing up in a city like?"

"What do you mean? Didn't you live in cities when you were in the Army?"

"I lived on base during my enlistment. Unless I was a tourist, I was at the bars conveniently located right outside of base."

"Ah, I see." She frowned like she was trying to come up with an adequate description. "It was normal. I don't know how else to describe it. Moore's different, but it's not. Stores aren't open as late, there's less variety in shopping, but I can still get what I need."

"How'd you get into swimming?" Dillon sensed if he didn't ask questions, she'd offer nothing else.

"My school had a swim team, and normally it's an expensive sport because you're paying for pool time, but they had hardship scholarships. I was a good swimmer so the school was happy to help me out. I swam until I graduated with my bachelor's. After that, I was burned out, which was good because I couldn't afford it."

She stated it so plainly. He knew guys who'd lost their *whole* identity when their football glory days were over. "How'd you pay your way through college besides the scholarship?"

"Retail jobs on the weekends and evenings. When I got into grad school, I worked as a teaching assistant. And loans. More than a few, and they'll be with me for a while before I can pay them off."

Again, she was matter-of-fact.

"You're paying for student loans, your dad's living, and your house?"

"I'm renting the house. When my loans are paid off, I can consider buying."

"Do you hear from your mom at all?"

Her expression froze. "No."

"Is that all I'm going to get?"

She gave him a hesitant smile. "It's not something I like to talk about, but really, there is nothing *to* talk about. She left saying she couldn't stand living with my dad anymore. He tried to hold it together after she left, but eventually—"

"Well hello, Elle."

Both of them jerked their attention to the man who'd stopped as he was walking by. He was smiling, but his gaze was jumping between them.

"Mr. Torkelson," Elle sounded pleased to see the man, but her rigid posture said otherwise.

"Rodney, please. Even at the office you can just call me Rodney."

"Are you enjoying a night out also?" she asked.

He beamed. "Me and the wife came to celebrate our twenty-fifth anniversary."

"Congratulations." Elle made introductions.

"Dillon, nice to meet you." Rodney stretched his hand out. Dillon firmly shook it, echoing Rodney's words. "You're one of the Walker boys that farm north of town?"

"Are we infamous?"

Rodney chuckled. "No, I was raised here so I knew your dad and uncles. They were a bit ahead of me in school."

"Then they're responsible for all the rumors."

"Absolutely. I'd better get back to the missus." He nodded at both of them, his mouth tightening briefly when he looked at Elle. "You two have a good night."

Dillon brought his attention back to Elle and the crease in her forehead. "He seems nice."

"He is. He's notorious for being very strict, holding his counselors to high standards."

"Like not dating their clients."

She pushed her plate to the side, worry apparent in her expression.

"It'll be okay, Elle. You did the right thing." He understood her dilemma. "How else would we have met?" he uttered quietly.

Right or wrong, the moment they met, she had become more to him than a counselor. More than a sexy woman he was interested in bedding.

She was the one.

If he could get her past her hang-ups about her dad, about work, she'd see it, too.

"We could have run into each other at the grocery store." She scowled and folded and refolded her napkin.

"How many men do you strike up a conversation with when you're buying milk?"

A shadow crossed her face. "Not milk. Ice cream, maybe,"

she muttered. "You promised me a date night and you mentioned dancing."

She wanted to lighten the mood; he'd oblige. "Hell, yes. There's even a live band playing tonight."

"I haven't seen a live band play in forever. Is all they play country music?"

"In Moore? Probably."

She nibbled on her lip before confessing, "I don't know how to dance...country."

Putting his hand over his heart, he feigned shock. "It just so happens, I'm an excellent teacher."

She cocked a brow at him. "Indeed?"

"But I have a fee."

A blush crept up her face. "I can't imagine what you charge."

Elle wasn't getting off that easy, literally or figuratively. "I'd like to show you around our operation."

She mulled it over, like paying with sex would've been a better option. "Don't you have your Grandma Agnes visit tomorrow?"

"We can go out in the morning and I'll bring you back to town when I go see Gram. I planned to bring her dinner so we'll have more of the day for sightseeing."

Her expression finally eased and she smiled. "Deal."

SUNDAY MORNING, Elle held onto the oh-shit handle as the truck bumped along the road. Deliciously sore already, she didn't want to add to it.

Their date night ruined her for upcoming dates. Spinning around the dance floor, at the mercy of where Dillon twirled her was the most she'd cut loose in...ever. An aphrodisiac to be in his arms, held close, moving their hips in time to the slower melodies. Her feet had hurt by the end of the night and she hadn't cared one bit. When they had gotten back to her place, they bee-lined to her bedroom where her feet weren't an issue.

Dancing and sex and Dillon. A lethal combination to her heart.

He swerved to miss a rough section in the already bumpy road.

"I can see why you need a pickup," she commented.

"There's been many times one of us has had to get pulled out. Only, the shit we get from the rescuing cousin is enough to keep us from being too careless the next time."

"Don't your tractors ever get stuck?"

"Yep. And it's a pain in the ass."

"How do you pull them out?"

He grinned. "Get a bigger truck." He turned off the narrow road that was actually only two dirt tracks in the grass onto an approach that stopped before a wire fence. "I'm actually showing you the cattle first. Nothing like a few furry calves to soften a woman's heart."

She peered out the window. "This might be a stupid question then. Where are the cows?"

He pointed toward a copse of trees. "Cash's house sits over there. The cattle only use this pasture in the winter so they've been moved already, but I can show you more of our properties' layout from this vantage point."

It hadn't been a long drive, but her muscles protested. She got out and stretched.

Dillon held a length of barbed wire up and pushed the rest of the fence down. "Ladies first. Watch out for cow patties."

She crawled through the fence, counting it as a first for her. Dillon pushed all the wire down and stepped over it all.

She wasn't brave enough for that, nor did she have the long legs to pull it off.

He gestured to the stretch of land behind Cash's property. "See how it dips down through the pasture. That makes it good for winter, along with the spring fed pond." She spotted the glimmering blue he indicated. "Then Cash doesn't need to haul hay so far to feed them."

"How do you move them?"

"Old-fashioned cattle drive, honey," he drawled in a Southern accent. "We all help with moving, surround the herd on horseback and steer them where we want them to go."

"That sounds so cool." And *smokin'* hot.

His lopsided grin reflected how much he enjoyed it. "It's one of my favorite times of the year. I love riding horses. Plan to get a couple next year, but I have to fix the fence around the pasture behind my house."

"I thought that was all farmland."

"Much of it is. There's several acres fenced off where we had horses growing up."

A shout caught their attention. A guy on horseback rode their way.

"Cash?" she guessed.

Dillon's mouth flattened. He curtly waved at the rider. "I'll show you the rest before he gets here." He wrapped an arm around her and turned them. Another cluster of trees sat in the distance with farmland as far as the eye could see. "Aaron works these sections."

The rounded tops of silver grain bins poked above the trees in the direction he pointed.

"I bet it's gorgeous in the summer." Hints of green along the land teased the eye. She imagined the beauty shone when trees leafed out and the pastures bloomed with wildflowers.

"Late summer is even better. Wheat fields are golden and

sunflowers face the sun. A couple local photographers call every year to find out where the best sunflower shots are. We let them come out, don't charge them anything."

"Do you get deals when you have portraits done?"

His eyebrows shot up. "I haven't had a formal picture taken since my senior year of high school. And that one they take at the start of basic training, but my freshly shaved head ruined that experience."

Chuckling, she turned toward a horse's chuff. Cash had arrived and, wow. Like Dillon and Brock, he was quite attractive, but the easy smile and casual attitude made him approachable. And she bet a lot of ladies approached him.

A navy-blue baseball cap with the logo of the Walker Five business complemented blue eyes a shade lighter than Dillon's. He wore a gray sweatshirt and worn jeans with boots similar to Dillon's—not quite work boots, but not cowboy boots.

Cash swung down from the horse who was interested in nibbling the new growth. This close together, the resemblance between the cousins was astounding; they could be mistaken for brothers.

"I was checking on the calves and noticed you driving up."

"Everything okay?" Dillon scratched the neck and ears of Cash's horse, more amiable to the creature than to his cousin.

"We have a heifer who's carrying late. She should be popping it out any day. Call me relieved she decided the snowstorm wasn't the time to calve."

Elle attempted to follow the conversation. Dillon elaborated. "A heifer is a first-time mom. She's overdue, and since she's never birthed before, she requires closer monitoring. There can be complications or she may even reject the calf."

She faced Cash. "So you're like a bovine midwife?"

Cash's blue eyes shot wide and Dillon barked out a laugh.

The horse lifted her head, but lost interest and went back to nuzzling through the grass.

Feeling foolish, she hoped Cash wasn't insulted by the comparison.

Dillon rescued her again. "Yes, Elle, Cash is our resident midwife. He knows more about birthing calves than anyone in the county."

Cash reached out a hand to shake Elle's. "I should be humble and deny it, but producing cattle is my career. It's my job to be good. Nice to meet you, Elle."

As attractive as he was, she felt no chemistry, no spark, when his hand touched hers. Likewise for him, if she read him right. Cash could have woman issues, but trying to steal his cousin's girl wasn't one of them.

From Dillon's proprietary hand on the small of her back, he was taking precautions.

"Is there room in your schedule for riding a horse next weekend?" Dillon asked.

A couple of seconds ticked by before she realized he was asking her. "Me? Oh. I've never…" The mellow mare snuffing and swiping her tail seemed harmless enough. Elle had always wanted to ride a horse. "Would it be okay?"

"Absolutely." He addressed Cash. "Mandrell would be a good one for Elle, don't ya think?"

"Oh yeah. She's older, doesn't spook easy. A good horse for teaching."

Elle eyed the coarse hair rippling in front of her. Tentatively, she stretched out a hand to gently pet down the long, graceful neck. "Is this Mandrell?"

"This is the number one female in my life, Patsy Cline." Cash's expression turned rueful as he scratched her ears and under her halter. "Once you get a saddle on her, she's about as compliant as Mandrell. It's the five minutes before that makes life interesting."

Getting braver, Elle stroked her face. Patsy Cline raised her head, the munching of grass getting ground between large teeth flexed the muscles under Elle's hand. "Do you only have mares?"

"Mares and geldings," Dillon answered. "Travis has a stallion, but with their sometimes aggressive temperament, we have to keep them away from the geldings. Unless we want a foal, he can't be pastured with the mares, either."

It was a whole different life they lived out here in the country. "Geldings are...?"

"Neutered, often calmer, but not always."

Cash leaned with one hand resting on the saddle, the other on his hip. "Let me know who you're riding next weekend Dillon and I'll get them in the barn. Tack's in the same place and ready to go."

"Appreciate it."

Farm talk and cow updates passed between the two of them. Elle listened, fascinated. This was a business. They were relatives, but they passed along information rapidly and succinctly like she and her coworkers did during their weekly meetings.

Dillon loosened up the longer he was around Cash. It was obvious they'd been close once. It could happen again if they talked and repaired their friendship before it tore apart any more of their lives.

"Any news on who stole your truck yet?" Cash's question darkened the mood.

"None. The storm put all of that on hold. Anyone been poking around your place?"

Cash shook his head. "We'll have to discover who it is to figure out why they targeted you. Or vice versa."

"Brock thought someone was checking out his place earlier this week."

That was the first Elle had heard about it. If the same

person had wrecked Dillon's truck, the behavior was almost guaranteed to escalate. What would happen next?

Cash toed his boot into the ground. "No shit? But no damage done?"

Dillon shook his head. "I mean to grab some estimates for equipping our property with security cameras and bring them to our next meeting."

Blowing out a breath, Cash shook his head, eyes stormy. "Won't be cheap. But if it's not this, it'll be something else. I agree, it's something we could use." With little effort, Cash swung up onto Patsy Cline. The creak of leather from the saddle wasn't enough to distract Patsy from her snack. "She loves to eat. A girl after my own heart. I'll let you two get back to the tour."

Regret etched into Dillon's features as he watched Cash ride off. His emotions were plain to decipher. He missed his best friend, but he was still too angry with him to open a line of conversation that didn't pertain to business.

"You two must've raised some serious hell when you were younger." She winced at her horrible attempt to lighten the mood.

Dillon flashed her an easy smile and wrapped his arm around her waist, leading her to the fence line. "We were good at not getting caught. Next stop is the small lake we fish at, then back to my place for lunch."

The way his voice dropped an octave suggested she would get more than food. And it accomplished his goal of switching topics. She leaned into him, allowing him the distraction. It was a beautiful day; she didn't want it to change.

CHAPTER 19

*E*lle had a free hour before lunch and used it to catch up on some notes and scan her afternoon appointments. It was only Wednesday, but it felt like three weeks should have passed.

Her first riding lesson was Saturday and she anticipated it like a five-year-old did Christmas. A real horse. Don't all little girls dream of riding a horse? With her very own cowboy—kind of. He was hotter than any cowboy she'd ever seen.

A knock caught her attention. "Come in."

Her boss entered, closing the door behind him. His expression serious. Dread settled over her.

"Elle, it was nice to see you out the other night."

"Yes, it was great seeing you, too." She recognized where the conversation was going.

"As you may have heard, the Walker boys are well known in town." Mr. Torkelson drew a deep breath. "So you understand when I remembered seeing Dillon's name on some insurance paperwork a few weeks ago, I...checked to see who his counselor was."

I did nothing wrong. I did nothing wrong. Maybe if she kept chanting those words, she'd believe them. "I'm sorry I didn't come to you earlier. We had two sessions together, and when it was clear he was interested in me, I informed him I could no longer be his counselor. We didn't start seeing each other until weeks later." Barely two weeks.

He gave her a disappointed look. "He hasn't been back since."

"I've been encouraging him," she said quietly, forcing herself to maintain eye contact. She clenched her hands on her lap, one thumb rubbing frantic circles on the other hand.

"Elle… You understand it's against company policy to see our clients personally."

"I understand. It's why I ended our sessions." Her voice remained steady. If she didn't sound guilty, he wouldn't think she violated company rules.

From his troubled expression, she wasn't in the clear yet. "How did you know when things were moving to a different level? Did you see him outside of work?"

She shook her head, maybe a little too hard. "After the first session. I gave him my recommendations for who to transfer to, but he was adamant that he wasn't going to see anyone else. Very insistent that he didn't need to be here in the first place."

"Then how did you two start dating?"

"His grandma is in the nursing home where my father was admitted. He was there visiting his grandma, we got to talking…" It was all she could do to keep her voice from wavering. "And that's all it was for a while, but eventually…"

God, what else could she say? It all sounded incriminating.

As he considered her story, she planted her hands on her desk so as not to wring them.

"I don't like it, Elle. You're new here. For this to happen so quickly after you were hired…" He blew out a gusty sigh. "It's a small town, these things happen. I'll give you the benefit of the doubt, but," he pinned her with a hard stare, "it'll prolong your probationary period. I'm going to extend it another six months."

Her heart sank. No raise. But she still had her job.

She forced a smile. "Of course, Mr. Torkelson. I'm sorry I didn't approach you earlier when I suspected it might be a problem."

He left her office. Elle blinked back the tears welling in her eyes. She'd finally relaxed and started enjoying her time with Dillon, forgetting all the reasons why seeing him was a bad idea.

One had been the threat to her employment, and she'd faced Mr. Torkelson. Two was the alcohol. Except for the beer in Dillon's fridge, she hadn't seen the drinking problem his family was worried about. If she had, she'd have ended things by now. The delay of a raise—well, things were tight, but she was making ends meet.

Vacillating between dating him or not had to stop. He'd been more than patient, it was her turn to go out on a limb.

"ELLE, meet Mandrell. She's a Paint who's been with our family for years."

Dillon led the mare by the halter to Elle. Her expression—pure awe and elation—was worth the sleepless night after not relaxing with a few beers before bed. The nightmares liked to hit when they were the most inconvenient and he'd refrained from drinking because of his date with Elle.

"She's gorgeous. Why do you call her a paint?" She spread her fingers out on the horse's neck, building her strokes until she was certain Mandrell accepted her.

"It's in the coloring. Paints have a spotting pattern. See how her white and dark coat colors blend."

He loosely tied the halter strap to the stall in the barn. Cash had brought the horses into the barn earlier in the morning so Dillon wouldn't have to coax them out of the pasture. "I'll be right back." He handed Elle a grooming brush. "Brush her back down for me, please."

The tack was stored in the corner of the barn. Dillon chose a smaller saddle that belonged to Cash's younger sister.

"Here's your first lesson." He handed Elle the saddle. She grabbed it, hefting the weight, inspecting the stitching. He held up a square piece of fabric. "The saddle blanket goes on first. It'll protect her back and soak up sweat."

He laid the blanket in place and lifted the saddle from Elle's grasp. Tossing it over the blanket, he wiggled it into place and showed her how to tighten the cinch strap.

"She's holding her breath, doesn't like it snug. But it needs to be, or the saddle'll slide around, and you'll go with it."

He held Elle's rapt attention all the way through saddling the mare. He couldn't put his finger on it, but something had shifted between them—for the better. Her smiles came easier and she was more open to him.

"LeDoux's turn. He's technically my horse, but it's better for him to stay with the other horses. He's young enough to think he's the boss."

"How do you come up with their names?"

Dillon opened the stall. LeDoux whinnied, Mandrell answered, and the horses outside the barn chimed in. "Old country singers our grandparents and parents listened to. You've heard of Patsy Cline?" Elle nodded, backing up while he led LeDoux out of the stall. "Barbara Mandrell and the Mandrell sisters, Chris LeDoux?"

She chuckled, reaching out to pet LeDoux's neck, but he jerked his head up and down. Elle snatched her hand back.

"It's all right, Elle. He's being stubborn. I'll give you some goodies to feed him and you'll be his new best friend."

Dillon trotted back to the corner to collect his tack. Elle helped him saddle the roan. He let her do much of it by herself to get hands-on experience, while he had his hands on her.

Elle stepped back to evaluate their handiwork. "What other country-star horses do you have?"

"Brock keeps his horse, Hank Senior, in the same pasture. My uncle, Brock's dad, loved Hank Williams, Sr. Aaron's old horse died last year, he'd had her most of his life. He's discussing with Travis plans for breeding one of his mares, Reba or Crystal Gayle."

"Will the new generation have contemporary country names?"

"Never know. Aaron loves him some Carrie Underwood. Or we could start a new trend and do movie stars or something." He handed Mandrell's lead rope to Elle. They guided the horses out of the barn.

Cash met them outside. "Hey, Dillon. The weather's supposed to stay nice. Perfect night for grilling. Travis's girl is hanging out with him. I'll call the others. Whaddya say? We'll do it here. I already took steaks out."

Elle squinted in the sun, smiling at Cash. Not the way Dillon saw most women gaze at him, but a good-natured greeting. He wanted to turn the invitation down, things between him and Cash were far from settled. For him at least; Cash seemed clueless. But if he turned the grilling party down, his cousin would insist, things would get awkward.

"If Elle's okay with it, we'll be there."

Elle's smile faded slightly as she gauged Dillon's reaction before answering. He gave her a slight nod. Cash was oblivious to the exchange.

"Sure." Her gaze flicked back to Dillon, searching for reassurance that she'd answered correctly.

Cash clapped his hands together. "I'd better clean some house. Hey Dil, if you go riding in the west pasture, can you inspect the fence line for me? I haven't made it out there yet."

Because he was wasting too much time at the bar picking up women. Even when Dillon slept in late, he still got all his work done.

"Will do." Dillon waited for Cash to leave before he turned to Elle. It gave him a chance to wipe the disappointment off his face. Elle was too astute to not notice. "Ready to mount?"

"Is there a special way?"

"You're on Mandrell's left, so put your left foot in the stirrup, grab the saddle horn, and haul your sweet ass up."

Despite her dubious look, she followed his directions. A triumphant smile accompanied a shimmy to situate herself in the seat of the saddle.

He grabbed her foot, moving it back until only the ball of her foot rested in the stirrup. "You never want to shove your whole foot in or it'll get caught if you need to dismount quickly. You're not wearing boots with a heel, but if you learn to ride like this, it won't be a problem in running shoes."

He swung up on LeDoux and held up the reins with his left hand. She mimicked his hold on her reins. "Now we ride."

Elle caught onto the commands riding next to him. They traveled through ditches, turning down prairie roads where they had complete privacy.

"This is amazing." Elle's face flushed from the cool breeze and her exuberance. "I'm riding a horse. Like, a *real* horse. I thought it'd be different than I'd imagined, but it's so much more."

Dillon chuckled. "If you took riding lessons, you'd be in a more controlled environment, with limited freedom controlling the animal. That's not a bad thing, but this is Mandrell's territory. She'll teach you to ride better than an instructor. Trust her instincts, but don't let her ride all over you."

They rode with only the sounds of nature and the horse's steps. Dillon led them to the fence Cash wanted him to look at. "When we're done inspecting this, we'll take a break, and head back to clean up for dinner."

"Are you certain you'll be okay tonight?"

He frowned. "Yeah, why?"

"You'll be around Cash."

"The others will be there."

"Have you and Cash talked about anything other than business since you returned home?"

"No." Why did she insist on ruining their lovely day with the topic of Cash?

"You need to."

"Well, tonight's not the night." He'd spoken with more force than intended.

She leveled him with a measured stare, but he ignored it. Feared he'd lash out at her again.

Urging LeDoux into a trot, he continued inspecting the fence, noting any areas that needed repair before the cattle were herded back in. He spun LeDoux around to Elle catching up. She was a natural on horseback, her body swaying side to side with Mandrell's steps.

"There's a pile of rocks we dug out of the field up ahead. Otherwise known as organic chairs to you city girls."

He received a guarded smile from her. Determined to ease the tension between them, he continued chatting until they reached the break area. After dismounting, he tied off his lead rope to a fence post. Elle did the same, not waiting for instruction.

He pulled her into his arms. "I'm sorry. I don't want my issues with my cousin clouding our afternoon. Or our night."

She cupped his face. "It'll cloud more than that if you keep ignoring it—and him."

Catching her lips, he deepened the kiss as if he could convince her nothing was wrong.

/ CHAPTER 20

$\mathcal{E}$lle laughed at a joke Cash cracked. She stood at Dillon's side while he talked with Brock and Cash entertained her. If any eligible woman in Moore could see her now, they'd waste away in envy.

Another tall, good-looking man entered the kitchen. He had coppery hair and eyes that appeared blue at first, but as he came closer, she saw flecks of green rimming the irises. She couldn't remember which cousin he was from the picture when Dillon had been describing them all.

Nodding to the others, he zeroed in on her. "You must be the Elle I've heard so much about."

"Guilty." He didn't have a girl with him so he must be—"Aaron?"

"Aww," he drawled, "I always knew I was Dillon's favorite. Talks about me all the time, does he?"

"Not nearly as much as you talk about yourself," Dillon chimed in.

Elle was content to stand back and watch the men chat. They were all each other's friends and family. Something she'd never experienced—neither having a lifelong friend nor a family member she was so close to. These guys all had each other, plus their own siblings.

But she was in the mix now. Getting to know people, thanks to Dillon's influence, and not just his relatives. She smiled at the memory of her chatting up Betsy during their Mental Health Wednesday tradition.

Movement out the window turned her head. A fifth pickup parked in line with the others. Two people were in the cab. The man who must be Travis and a woman were talking. From the flailing of her arms, she seemed upset. She got out of the pickup and slammed the door.

Definitely upset.

Travis followed her, his hands held out, pleading for her understanding.

She wasn't having it.

Elle watched in fascination as the woman composed herself before entering Cash's house. By the time she and Travis entered, they acted civil. Guess Dillon and Cash weren't the only ones pretending nothing was wrong.

After introductions and greetings, Cash fired up the grill. Elle tried to strike up a conversation with Michelle, Travis's fiancée. It was like talking to a sheet in the breeze. The girl's mind was somewhere else.

Thank the lucky stars, Cash started pulling steaks off the grill. Elle jumped into help set the table, eager to do any task that prevented her from chatting with Michelle.

"Want a beer, water, or soda?" Dillon spoke quietly in her ear.

"Water, please."

Dillon reappeared with a bottle of water for her and a can of beer for himself.

Elle held her tongue, glancing briefly between him and the beer can. He was a grown man and they were surrounded by people.

Dinner was filled with talk and laughter and absolutely excellent steak. Elle never grilled herself, rarely ordered it eating out; it made the gathering extra special.

Until Dillon cracked open a second beer.

Talking grew louder, jokes became rowdier, and Elle's gut hurt from laughing. It was the only thing that covered the sinking feeling that her relationship with Dillon was taking a different course than she'd thought this morning.

He was on his third beer.

Clean up. She could help clean up, then she needed to head home. Her home. She couldn't overnight it with Dillon tonight. She'd just committed to giving their relationship a chance, no easy decision. Every crack of a can opening sunk her optimism further.

Walking to the kitchen with an armload of dishes, she noticed Michelle standing by the dishwasher, her back to Elle.

"Is it full, or is there room for more?"

Michelle jumped, wiping at her eyes before she opened the door of the dishwasher. "No. Nope. Load it up."

The girl kept her back to Elle.

"Is everything okay?"

Nodding vigorously, back still turned, Michelle sniffled. "Just fine. Got something in my contact and my eye's watering up a storm."

Elle didn't need her degree to read through that.

Raised voices blasted in from the other room. She and Michelle raced out.

"I'm just saying, you're *telling* us that's what you're planning," Dillon shouted, "but what are you really going to do Cash? You're not known for following the rules."

"Bullshit, Dillon," Cash hollered back. "You got a problem with me, say it."

"I don't have to!" Dillon roared. "You know exactly what you did!"

"We aren't in fucking Iraq anymore, and you don't outrank me. You're in my house so you can get the fuck out."

Elle turned the corner. Travis jumped to stand in front of Michelle as if protecting her, Brock and Aaron flanked the two men who were standing nose-to-nose yelling.

Dillon's head whipped toward her, his eyes blazing, jaw grinding, fists clenched.

Cash mirrored him, until he saw her and Michelle being blocked by Travis. "Fuck. I'm sorry."

"Sorry doesn't always cut it when you hurt someone. But lying suits you just fine," Dillon spit out.

Cash's gaze spun back to Dillon. "Don't be an angry drunk."

"Fuck you. I don't know why no one questions your whoring ways, but every time I turn around, someone's bitching about my drinking, thinking I've got fucking PTSD."

Elle couldn't help but feel hurt. His umbrella statement had included her.

"They bitch about your drinking because you don't get your ass into the field until damn near noon. At least I'm not sitting on my couch blaming everyone else for coming home and feeling like shit."

Dillon stood inches from Cash, his finger shoved into Cash's chest. "I wouldn't feel that way if you had done what you were supposed to. I'm not the one who got someone killed."

Aaron and Brock inched closer, ready to pull the two angry men off each other.

"How the fuck would you know what happened? You just assumed it was all my fault."

"It always is." Dillon stalked toward Elle, grabbing her hand, pulling her behind him out the door.

The force of the stare from the others rested heavy between her shoulder blades. How she hated the pitying looks for the poor girl who had to leave with the drunk guy who was being an ass.

He dug his keys out of his pocket.

"Dillon, I'll drive."

He reared back like she'd told him to go to hell. She couldn't promise that wasn't how the night would end.

"It's less than a mile home. I'm fine."

"You've been drinking." How many times had she had this conversation? Wrestled her father for his keys while he could barely stand on his own two feet?

The muscle in Dillon's jaw flexed, he glowered at her. Finally, he handed her the keys and climbed into the passenger side of his truck.

Hauling herself into the driver's seat, she refused to glance at him. His anger clogged the cab. He was probably angry at the world, like her father always was. Dwelling on all the ways he'd been wronged. Blaming everything that had happened in Iraq that he refused to talk about on Cash.

During the strained two-minute drive back to his place, neither of them spoke. She pulled into his garage but left the door open so she could get out to her car.

"You're leaving?" His expression mixed indignation with misunderstanding.

She handed him back his keys and got out. "I'm not going to stay here when you've been drinking."

"*Three* beers, Elle," he said, following her. "That's all."

She put her hand up to stop him. "You've had five and I've had this conversation too many times in my life. I don't ever want to have again it."

"What is that supposed to mean?"

Tears welled. She heard her dad's voice, swearing about how little he'd had to drink, slurring his words the entire time. "It means I don't want to have it again. I never should have gotten this involved with you, Dillon. I almost lost my job, I lost my raise, and I can't do it anymore. I *refuse* to sacrifice any more of my life for alcohol." She choked on a sob, rushing to her car.

In a daze, she started her car and swung it around. Through her tears, she saw Dillon in her rearview mirror, looking as confused and distraught as she felt.

WHAT THE FUCK was that ringing?

Dillon groaned and rolled over, landing with a thud on the floor as his sorry ass was dumped out of the couch.

Fuck, I didn't drink that *much.* He hauled himself to his hands and knees, knocking over several cans that clanked and rolled under him.

Maybe I did.

The fight with Elle. She'd been disgusted with him, couldn't get away fast enough. He'd come inside, thrown a few things, punched his table, busted up his damn hand. Then he'd had more to drink…because the damage had been done. Why not? Everyone thought he was an alcoholic anyway.

She'd broken up with him and left.

He rested his forearms on the edge of the couch and laid his head on them. With eyes closed, the world still spun.

The high-pitched ringing continued.

He pushed himself up. Balancing himself on his feet was harder than he anticipated. He looked at the time. Middle of the damn night.

What was that noise?

He ambled to the kitchen. His heart slammed to his feet, the fog in his mind blowing clear.

An orange haze lit up his kitchen. He ran to the window to find the source.

Flames licked along the sides of his shop, the siding already burned and blackened.

Reaching in his pocket for his phone—it wasn't there.

His heart hammering, he searched frantically. He needed to call the fire department. It lay by on the floor by the couch where he recalled in utter dismay that he'd been drunk dialing Elle.

For fuck's sake. He'd screwed up bad.

It took him three tries, bogged down by beer and amped up by adrenaline, to dial 9-1-1.

He gave them the information while staggering out of his house. The blaze reached as high as the roof. Heat singed his face even as he stood across the yard, helpless to watch. No fire extinguisher he owned would dent that fire.

Would he lose all the equipment? Insurance only went so far. He'd already taken a minor financial hit replacing his pickup.

He couldn't do nothing. Racing into the garage, he grabbed a garden hose and hooked it up. Getting as close as he dared and as near as the hose would allow, he aimed and sprayed. Did it do any good? Probably not, but he was doing something.

Thick smoke in the air clogged his airway. He covered his mouth with his shirt, tasting nothing but ash. His bare feet burned as if scorched from the heat.

Several minutes later, the sirens of the rural fire department filled the night. He hoped it was enough to wake Brock. Calling his cousins was high on his to-do list, but not until every damn spark was put out.

The patrol car pulled into his yard before the fire engine.

A young deputy Dillon had never met got out. "Sir, I'm going to have to ask you to move back to safety."

Dillon glared at him, his water spray aimed at the shop, sweeping back and forth. "You know I'm not going to listen, right?"

"Mr. Walker—"

A red engine rolled in and firemen jumped out. Dillon was as relieved to see them as he was to hear the sirens of another engine on the way.

Once they had their massive hoses going full force, Dillon finally stepped back.

The other set of sirens didn't belong to a fire engine, but an ambulance.

"What are they doing here?" Dillon asked the young cop. He wasn't going anywhere.

"Standard procedure. All three departments respond to fires."

Dillon nodded numbly, collapsing on the steps of his porch. Whatever Deputy What's-his-name asked him, he answered. The EMTs hung out next to them. An older no-nonsense EMT interrogated him. Dillon brushed her concerns off. If his skin was beet red from the heat, he didn't care, he wasn't leaving.

Brock's pickup skidded into the yard, parking by the ambulance. He got out, his mouth open in disbelief. Dillon knew exactly how he felt, what was running through his mind. *How? Why? How much were we going to lose? And again—how?*

"Wha—" Brock couldn't finish, swinging back to stare at the crumbling shop.

It was Brock's turn to get interrogated by the deputy. Brock's presence was reassuring, but the deputy could distract Dillon as long as he needed. Dillon's headspace wasn't ready to deal with his cousins' reactions.

Aaron arrived next, then Travis. The only no-show was

Cash and Dillon wasn't surprised. Their drama didn't have any place around the high emotions of the fire.

The firemen stayed until daybreak brightened the sky, until no more embers flared. They stomped around, ensuring that was the end of it. The fireman Dillon had seen ordering the others around beckoned the deputy over.

Dillon got up to follow but was ordered to sit tight.

Asshole. He sat back down and pressed his fingertips to his throbbing temples.

"What the hell happened?" Aaron asked.

"I heard the shop's fire alarm going off." His dad had been so proud of that thing, had installed it himself. It was an industrial alarm loud enough to wake the dead. It was the headache icing on his brain.

Travis squatted down, staring him dead in the eye. "Are you drunk?"

Dillon scowled back. "No." *Not anymore.*

"Where were you when you heard the alarms?" Aaron sounded like the officer when he'd interrogated Dillon.

"Asleep on the couch. Now back off."

"Where's Elle?" Brock asked.

"Went home last night," Dillon mumbled.

Travis rose to his feet, his attention never leaving him. "Were you asleep on the couch, or passed out on it?"

Dillon stood, refusing to be ganged up on by his cousins. "If I was passed out, I wouldn't have woken up when the alarms went off!"

"How long had they been going off?" Aaron folded his arms on his chest, his face tight with anger. "How long did the fire burn freely before you *woke up*?"

"I woke up with the alarms!"

"How high were the flames by the time you got out here, Dillon?" Travis asked. Dillon and Travis glowered at each other until Travis nodded. "Thought so."

"Did Elle break up with you, is that why you were drinking?" Brock spoke quietly, like he was afraid of the answer.

"No. She was just pissed about my fight with Cash and went home."

"Are you sure that's all she was upset about?" Travis was so aggravatingly calm. "I heard her take your keys from you."

"Do you want to tell my why you and Michelle were fighting? No. Because it's none of my business, correct?"

Travis spoke evenly. "My argument with Michelle didn't make me drink until I passed out and let our shop burn down."

"Fuck you."

"Exactly. I'm going home to my fiancée, who didn't leave me because I'm a drunk, sad idiot who starts shit at a family get-together."

Travis spun and walked away. Dillon lunged for him. Aaron and Brock grabbed him by the arms. The deputy saw the altercation and started for them, but Dillon backed off until the cop's attention went back to the fireman.

"This is what you're going to do." Aaron's vice grip around his arm enraged him, but Dillon didn't physically react. Didn't need to be hauled away in cuffs on top of everything else tonight. "You're going to sleep it off and we'll finish up with Deputy Olson."

"Do you think I can go in and sleep after this?" The pounding in his head was getting worse anyway.

"You can't stay out here and cause a fight," Brock replied.

"Quit making this all my fault."

"Take responsibility for what is." Brock let him go and waved him off in disgust as he stomped away.

Aaron leveled Dillon with the sternest look he'd ever seen. Usually Dillon was the one who doled out that look.

"Go inside. Clean yourself up." Aaron followed Brock.

The demolished shop provided the backdrop to where his

cousins were in discussion with Deputy Olson. Through the jagged holes in the walls, blackened, sooty equipment sat still smoking. How much had survived the heat, there'd be no telling for days.

He glanced down at himself. Still in his clothes from yesterday, he smelled like a bonfire and ached like he'd been through the burn pit. He trudged inside and stripped right inside the door. Considering whether to keep his pants and shirt seemed insignificant, but at the moment, it was all he controlled in his world. He dumped his clothing in the washing machine.

On his way to the bathroom, the mess of scattered beer cans greeted him from next to the couch. Ugh, that was a lot of cans. He couldn't face cleaning them up, not yet. He'd feel better after a shower.

When the bathroom light flicked on, he groaned. Squinting into the mirror, bloodshot slits peered back. He was dirty, smelly, and in too rough a shape to deal with the shit going on in his life.

A sharp knock on the bathroom door startled him.

"Yeah?"

"Deputy Olson talked to the firemen," Brock said through the door. "They said the fire marshal needs to inspect the shop, but it looks like arson."

Dillon closed his eyes and let his head fall back. Arson. Not only had he slept through the fire, but through someone *setting* the fire. If the arsonist had targeted his home, he might not have gotten out alive.

"So get some rest," Brock continued. "I mean it. When you get up, we'll have a meeting. I'll let you know what the Deputy needs from us."

"Okay."

His cousins picked up what Dillon's hung-over ass couldn't. When had their roles reversed? Dillon had been the one they'd all depended on to put out figurative fires, and tonight he'd been useless.

When he climbed into the shower, he stood under the spray, staring at the floor. He'd lost Elle over three beers.

You've had five...

He cupped his hands to collect water and splashed it on his face.

There were another eight cans lying on the floor in his living room.

He'd been an insensitive jerk. She'd opened up to him about her upbringing and he knew she hadn't scratched the surface with how much she'd been through. But he'd stubbornly decided he knew what was best, that everyone around him was wrong, and he'd drunk. Then almost fought Cash.

He leaned against the shower stall and let the water rain down on him.

God, he missed his best friend. He closed his eyes and saw that building blow, with Cash still inside.

He'd never known fear like that. And the awful guilt.

The thing between him and Cash festered, and again, Dillon hadn't listened to Elle.

He'd lost her. Lost Cash. And lost his shop and the all the equipment inside.

Standing here didn't get them back. Just proved how useless he'd become.

Dillon finished his shower, dried off, and collapsed on his bed.

Staring at the ceiling, his mind wouldn't shut down. He was supposed to be waking up to the most beautiful woman he'd ever met. Instead, he was alone in his bed. His cousins were outside thinking he was becoming a lost cause.

He'd sleep. Then he'd get his life in order.

CHAPTER 21

*E*lle's client wrapped up his diatribe about never being able to smoke weed again.

"Clinton, most addicts don't think it's fair to not be able to have the substance they're addicted to again."

"I know, but not even once in a while?" He fell quiet and she didn't respond. "Is everything going okay, Elle? You seem…"

Tired? Crabby? Depressed? Lonely? Pick one Clinton, you wouldn't be wrong. "I'm doing well, Clinton, thanks for asking." She steered the conversation back to what he could do to keep himself from having a toke, which in Clinton's case always led to a hit of the harder stuff.

When he left, Elle heaved a sigh of relief. It was only Monday, but at least the workday was d-o-n-e. She'd spent Sunday in tears, or trying not to cry around her dad. He'd sensed something was wrong, but no matter how subtly he'd probed, she'd never opened up. Burdening her dad with the breakup wasn't in his best interest and she'd always dealt with her problems on her own.

But for the first time in a very long time, she'd wanted to.

For a moment on Sunday night, when her dad had sat on a chair next to her to ask what was wrong, she'd flashed back to the months after her mom had abandoned them. Her dad hadn't crawled back into the bottle right away and he'd done his damnedest to see Elle through the turmoil.

God, the two of them. What a pair. What they'd been through together. Their life had changed more than once, but they were still weathering it together. But she doubted she'd ever lose that feeling, the constant, simmering anxiety, that he'd revert to his old coping mechanisms.

Heading home had wiped out any emotional stability she'd maintained at her dad's. The multitude of texts that decreased in coherency she'd received Saturday night proved she'd done the right thing. She thought a full workday of helping addicts would reinforce her decision. Her heart didn't agree with either line of thinking, and Elle suspected her brain disagreed, too.

Betsy knocked on her door and entered before Elle answered. "OMG, I heard about what happened at Dillon's place. Were you out there when it happened?"

Elle spun in her chair, a frown on her face. Her heart stuttered at the idea Dillon might be hurt. "No, what happened?"

Confused, Betsy elaborated. "The shop? Burned down?"

Elle eyes grew wide. "Dillon's shop burned down?"

"You didn't know?"

"We, uh…aren't seeing each other anymore." Watching her hands twist together, Elle avoided Betsy's incredulous gaze.

"*Whaaat?*" She sat down, scooting her chair closer. "I'm so sorry."

"I should've known it wouldn't work. I mean, I knew. We met because he was my client, after all."

Betsy canted her head, her expression curious. "He wasn't taking his problem seriously?"

Grateful her friend understood enough that Elle didn't have to spell it out, she nodded. Tears popped into her eyes. She hastily wiped them away. Before she knew it, she was pressed into Betsy's ample bosom for a bear hug.

Elle was caught between *I need to get the hell out of here* and *I really appreciate the comfort and want to stay awhile*, but Betsy released her before she had to decide.

"Dillon Walker's a good guy. He made you happy. Even when I didn't know you two were together, I noticed a difference in you." Betsy paused, choosing her words. "If he were to find recovery, would you give him a chance?"

Elle dabbed at her eyes with a tissue. "I-I—" She shook her head. "No. I promised myself for years, I'd never be with someone with an addiction." *Like my dad.*

"I understand." Betsy sat back in the chair. "You've never met my husband, but he and I met in a recovery group. Dillon reminds me a lot of him when we were younger."

Elle's hand dropped to her lap. Betsy's confession floored her—and wasn't making her feel better.

"He was into meth."

Elle's brows shot up.

"So was I."

Her mouth dropped open. She could maybe envision Betsy into alcohol, but hardcore drugs…?

Betsy chuckled. "I know, I know. Group isn't where we should be making love connections. We'd both been in recovery for a while before we clicked. It happens." Her mouth quirked. "I don't tell many people that, but hey, some things in life lead us toward counseling."

"Why did you tell me?"

Betsy sighed. "I don't want you to throw away a good thing because you're afraid. Give Dillon some time."

"Thank you for the advice." The slight edge in Elle's voice signaled the end of the conversation.

"Take care, Elle," Betsy said before she left.

Elle stared at her computer until the screen went to sleep.

Dammit, Betsy. She'd only known the vivacious woman since she'd started working, but Betsy was one of the most stable people she knew. And her family was beautiful. Elle hadn't met them, but Betsy brought in a new story every day, and her desk was a clutter of kid drawings and photographs.

Meth addicts. If they could work for a happy-ever-after, maybe… No, she couldn't deviate. It was her heart and her life she protected.

~

DILLON CHECKED THE TIME. "I need to get going, Gram."

He had to make it to Fargo in time for a meeting. The previous week, he'd gone to a Fargo AA meeting even with the arson situation, especially with the arson.

"They're no closer to finding out who set the fire?" Grandma Agnes asked.

"Nothing. It's been a month and we're no closer to knowing." They'd lost the big tractor. The smaller tractor and other attachments needed a lot of TLC, but it was cheaper than buying. He'd saved a ton of the tools, but it would be expensive replacing the rest.

"The guys and I are still cleaning up so we can build a new shop and set up all the security cameras." They had two cheap models aimed on the salvaged equipment and his house. "I don't get it. It's like a phantom's haunting me."

And Dillon didn't know when he'd strike next.

She rocked in her chair with a thousand-yard stare out the window. "I used to feel that way, too, out there." She chortled. "It's why I married your grandpa so quickly after—" Her smile died.

"After what, Gram?"

"Hmm? A shame the police have no idea."

"Tell me about it." Dillon stood. "I'm bringing Chinese next week for our lunch date. Be hungry."

"I'll be the envy of the low-sodium crowd." She rose to give him a kiss. "You look good, Dillon. And I'm sorry about Elle."

"Me, too." He returned her kiss.

The drive to Fargo was relaxing. Before, it used to drive him crazy. Now, it gave him time to think, and he thought he needed a new girl in his life. Maybe more than one.

CHAPTER 22

Five weeks had gone by. Elle's insides were no longer twisted in knots, just numb like her mind. Her routine never wavered. She went to work, ran errands, got groceries, visited her dad. Stayed far away from the nursing home part of the building so she wouldn't run into Grandma Agnes.

Tonight greeted her with a slight change in her nightly activities. She returned the gas nozzle to the pump. She'd paid at the pump, but it was Friday night. What the hell. A perusal of the goodies available inside might reveal something that *had* to come home with her.

Drifting down the coolers, she found nothing that sounded irresistible. She turned into the chocolate aisle. Gigantic bricks of milky goodness lined the top. Squatting down she tried to find something that wouldn't burn a whole weekend's worth of calories. Once the aquatic center opened, she'd swim an hour then tackle one of those monsters.

"I can't wait for you to meet her, Mama." A familiar voice drifted over the shelves. Elle froze, praying Dillon didn't turn down her aisle. "She'll meet you at the door, and you'll fall in love like I did."

Dillon had found someone new? Suddenly, candy held no appeal.

"Go ahead and make yourself at home. See you in a bit, Mama."

Elle stayed down. If she stood, she might be noticed.

"Elle?"

Damn. Rising, she strove to sound unaffected by what she'd heard. "Dillon." She tried to smile. No success, it was like her facial muscles had atrophied.

He glanced around, but no one was nearby. "I've been meaning to call you. I wanted to apologize." He shifted his gaze away, clearing his throat. "I'm sorry about how I acted."

Don't cry. Don't cry. Same ball cap, work boots, navy-blue sweatshirt. His blue eyes were clear and contrite, his hair freshly trimmed. For the new girl?

Civil. She could be civil until she collapsed in a puddle of tears at home. "I was sorry to hear about your shop." There. That was a good start.

His face clouded, his jaw tightened. "Yeah, it was pretty bad. But we're recovering. I'm back out in the field, trying to plant when the weather allows."

She missed the easy talk about his life's blood. She missed him.

A lot.

"Elle?"

He'd asked her a question? "What?"

He flashed her an easy smile. "I asked if you had anything fun planned for the weekend. My mom's coming down. I'm trying to talk her out of filling my freezer."

"Are you cooking then?" *Or is the new girl doing it for you?*

He shrugged. "A little more than I used to. Besides, it's getting nicer out. Grilling season."

Aaand there was the splash in the face back to reality. Events from the last grilling party soured her mood, reminding her of what it'd cost her.

Sensing the change between them, he held up a case of mineral water. "I'd better get going and meet Mama. It was nice seeing you, Elle."

This time, she succeeded at plastering on a smile. "Same here. Have a good weekend, Dillon."

He turned, then pivoted back. "Can I call you sometime?"

Yes! No! Omigod, what should she say? "I don't know if…" She couldn't bring herself to say the rest.

His expression turned…resigned. "I understand. See you later, Elle."

She gaped at his form walking away, wishing she could admire the fine view, but she was too torn up inside. He left. Just like that. The Dillon who'd pursued her so fervently was gone.

Her cravings were wiped out. She rushed out of the store empty handed. And ran right into a man's chest.

"Jesse!"

"We just keep running into each other." He grinned down at her.

"I guess." She attempted to side-step him, but he spun with her.

"Have you eaten yet? We can go grab a bite."

He was asking her out again? The childish part of her wanted to say yes. After all, Dillon was going home to someone else besides his mama. Responsible adulting won.

"I'm not hungry." Truth. "Thanks for offering." She continued to her car, feeling his eyes on her back the whole time.

Yes. She'd made the right decision. About Jesse at least. Climbing into her car, she glanced in the review mirror.

There was that truck again. She frowned, but brushed it off. Small towns.

~

"She's cute, isn't she?" Dillon laughed as he stood in his driveway with his mom. She was getting licked by an exuberant yellow lab. His dog circled Mama's legs, tail wagging ferociously.

Mama giggled, giving the dog a good scratch. "What did you name her again?"

"Dottie."

"And you said you got some cats, too?" Mama gave Dottie one more good scratch before lifting a couple of bags of groceries she'd brought for cooking "just a few meals."

He picked up the other ten bags. "Trixie and Dixie. Already fixed so I don't have to worry about batches of feral kittens."

Mama walked into the house. "Feral and kittens don't go together, but good idea. Kitties are so cute, it's hard to give them up. Where did you find them?"

"There were plenty of cats at the pound. I picked ones who looked like good mousers. Dottie I found in the county classifieds. Her owner was moving out of state, couldn't bring her with."

"I'm glad you have some company out here. I can't help but wonder why the sudden change, though." He helped empty the groceries from the sacks.

"Part of my recovery."

Mama stopped, her hand paused on a cupboard door.

"You and Dad were right. I have a problem. I drank my feelings, and I drank because I was lonely. Pets help with the loneliness. What's a farm without pets, anyway?"

She smiled and rounded on him, hugging him tight. "I was so worried about you."

"I know." He returned her embrace. "I'm sorry for causing you concern. I'm sorry you felt like you had to coddle me because I couldn't take care of myself."

"The day you were born, I realized I would worry every day of my life." They went back to unloading. "I don't dote on you because I think you can't handle it. I do it because I need to take care of my son. That'll never change."

"I left you and Dad for the Army." The words almost stuck in his throat. Until he said them aloud, he hadn't known how much it had eaten away at him. Coming home to a sick dad had planted a seed of guilt deep inside.

His mom blinked owlishly at him. "Why would you be sorry? We were so proud of you. Your father was as relieved you'd get to experience life off the farm as he was when you confirmed you were coming back. We always knew you'd return. And..."

"Mama?"

She shrugged, sadness shimmering in the depths of her hazel eyes. "Your dad and I were always grateful that the military paid for your education. Not that we wouldn't have made it happen," she finished hastily. "But, well, the financial burden of him being sick was easier to weather."

Huh. If he hadn't been working through his feelings and had talked with his mom, *really* talked, he wouldn't have carried the guilt for decades, letting it slowly destroy him. And he wouldn't have crawled inside a silver can and drowned.

She squeezed his elbow like she always did once he grew too tall to get his hair ruffled. "I'm glad you're getting help, improving your life."

"Same here. I almost lost everything before I opened my eyes." Literally, but the shop wasn't on the same level as Elle.

"Have you talked to her?" she asked softly.

"Half hour ago, as a matter of fact. Went as well as I could hope." His amends had seemed inadequate, but it was as far as he could get with her for now. His goal was to stick to the twelve steps and someday perhaps he could apologize proficiently. "Speaking of which, when are you going out with your friends?"

"They asked about tonight, but I wanted to hear your plans first."

"Go ahead. We'll grill burgers tomorrow night after I get in from the field." He needed to talk to someone, and if everything went well, he'd need the whole night.

With the last of the groceries put away, Mama picked up her overnight bag. "I need to text them and clean up. Don't wait up for me."

He grinned to himself. Mama Walker wasn't yet sixty. When his dad had retired and they'd moved closer to advanced healthcare, Mama had done the opposite and gone to work. She loved kids, found work in a school, and learned to live again after his dad passed away. He marveled at her strength.

He grabbed two cans from his fridge. Other than milk, the only beverage he had contained lemon-lime sparkling water. Within minutes, he pulled up at Cash's place.

He wasn't moving forward in life until he got this over with. Until he repaired what he could of his relationship with Cash. They'd always be cousins, but Dillon wanted his best friend back. Life was too damn lonely with no one to talk to. Something Elle had tried to get through to him.

The house was empty. The barn was the next likely spot to find Cash. Hitting the bars, searching for women, was the only time the guy quit working. They hadn't interacted since the night of the fight.

Cash was speaking quietly to a horse. Patsy Cline probably knew Cash better than any of them, heard all his secrets.

Stepping through the shadows, Dillon called out his cousin's name. They both hated being taken off guard after their deployments.

Cash's back was to him, red frayed ball cap pulled down low. He tossed the curry comb on the bench and took his gloves off. "Yeah?"

"We need to talk. About more than our fight."

Cash's head dropped. Dillon couldn't tell if it was in disgust or resignation.

"I already know that you think what happened was all my fault." Cash's voice was low. "And you'd be right." He braced his hands on the top of the bench as if waiting for Dillon's barrage.

Dillon walked around Patsy Cline, running his hand along her flanks to keep from spooking her. "I'm willing to hear the whole story."

It was a guess. An educated guess because he knew Cash better than anyone, he'd known he was lying when he'd recalled the event for their superiors. Since Dillon was being honest with himself, it was the main reason for why he was so angry with Cash. They'd been best friends, done everything together, and Cash hadn't trusted him with the truth.

He leaned against the bench. Cash hadn't moved.

"It was his fault, too. Daniels." Cash gave a sharp laugh. "Sometimes I wish I could bring him back from the dead so I could fucking strangle him."

Dillon chanced a glance at Cash. His mouth was set, eyes unfocused, shoulders held taut. He was back in Iraq.

"You were ordering us to fall back. He kept going, deeper into the building we were clearing. 'Just one more room,' he said. I had a bad feeling." Cash blew out a gusty breath and shrugged. "I couldn't let him go alone, I couldn't turn around and go back. By the time I decided to follow him…"

"He'd set off the IED." The explosion had rocked the ground Dillon stood on. He had been terrified he'd lost his cousin as dust blew out of every opening. And ashamed at his relief when he'd heard it wasn't Cash who'd died. It had been easier to blame Cash for everything.

Cash finally turned around. "I should've stopped him. Physically dragged his ass back."

"Daniels was…Daniels. Stuck in his head, easily distracted. It wouldn't have done any good." Cash nodded like he was being polite. Dillon knew how he felt, they both blamed themselves. "I think the same thing. I should've done more."

"Nah, man. You were by the book. Me and Daniels weren't. But…I didn't mess around in the field. I thought you knew that." Cash's accusation simmered in his crystal blue eyes.

He was right. Dillon should've known. Cash ran the ranch with extreme care and precision, unlike his personal life. It was the same in the military. But Dillon had let feelings of betrayal cloud his thinking, found fault in everything Cash had done since they returned.

"I was so damn angry. I knew you didn't report everything, didn't tell me everything…"

Cash looked away. "My report was precise."

"But didn't include everything."

"What could I say? 'Yes, sir, I think Daniels intentionally killed himself.'"

"You really think so?"

Cash nodded, his expression grim. "He'd been saying weird shit. Once, he'd even joked about how his life insurance would help his sister finish college."

"That's why you didn't tell anyone." Dillon's opinion of

Cash increased exponentially. To cast doubt on Daniels' death might've cost his family, and they'd already lost their son.

"I knew joining the Army was a bad decision the first day of basic training."

Dillon gaped at Cash. "You stayed in for *eight* years."

"Yep. Know why? I didn't know what else to do." He laughed with derision. "All I wanted to do was ranch, but Mom and Dad— So I stayed. I would've been fucked if we'd gotten stationed separately again."

Dillon stared at him. *Eight* years. Because he couldn't come home and work with cattle. —No wonder he hadn't earned rank like Dillon. He'd been biding his time, waiting until Dillon got out so he could take over ranching operations. Yet, Dillon had stayed in for Cash.

He closed his eyes for a heartbeat. Take responsibility for his own actions. Dillon had made his own choice to stay in. Maybe he'd understood better then that he hadn't been ready to come home.

"I'm sorry, Cash. It feels weak as hell, but I'm sorry."

"Yeah, me, too." Cash took his ball cap off, scratched his neck, and pressed the palms of his hands over his eyes. "Look at us. A couple of sorry bastards."

Dillon chuckled. He wasn't set straight with Cash yet, but they were headed in the right direction. They needed time and Cash needed his support.

"Have you eaten yet? Mama's in town, but she's out with friends."

Cash perked up. "Aunt Christy's here? Is she going to drop off some meals for me again?"

"She'd love to. I've limited her to ten meals for me."

"Sure, I could eat. Want to hit The Place?"

No, Dillon didn't. Mentally raw wasn't a good condition to go to the bar in. "How about a restaurant?"

Cash's puzzled expression changed to understanding. "Oh right. Brock said you'd quit drinking."

Dillon lifted a shoulder. "Right now it's easier not to be around it. I need to find other ways to relax."

"I don't think Dottie's going to be relaxing," Cash said wryly.

He agreed. "She's young yet, and bored being on her own. I might have to get another dog. I'm actually going to take her running in the mornings."

Cash developed a lopsided grin. "Going back to doing morning PT like in the Army?"

"Yep. I think it'll be good for me." *And help me sleep at night.*

"Maybe I'll go with you some time."

Something they could do together since Dillon had sworn off the bar scene and wasn't interested in dating.

Cash walked over to Patsy Cline to untie her. "Once Patsy's back in the pasture, I'll change clothes and head in. I'd better drive separate cuz…you know."

"Ever think of settling down?"

Cash cast him a droll look. "When I find someone who interests me for more than one night at a time, I'll think about it. I'm rooting for you and Elle, FYI."

"I wish she was, too," Dillon muttered, walking back to his truck.

CHAPTER 23

Elle woke up on the couch.

It was slightly after ten-thirty. She'd been woken up by the jingle of the nightly news.

Wild one right here, people.

And since she hadn't come home with any goodies, she was hungry. Her sparse I'm-feeling-sorry-for-myself supper had burned off long ago.

Would she even be able to go back to sleep? She was stuck deciding between going back to sleep or slogging to her bed using as little energy as possible so she could fall asleep in the proper place.

She sighed. If that was the hardest decision she faced, her life was beyond boring.

The weather would be on soon. She'd just wait. There was always reading in bed if she couldn't sleep.

Elle wrapped up her rowdy night by shutting the TV off when the weather portion was over. She shut the main lights off, and out of habit, she peeked out the curtains to check the street. It was something her dad had always done before bed.

She pulled away, her hand dropping, her heart rate

increasing.

That truck. The beat up one she'd first seen outside work. Then later that night when she'd gone out for Mental Health Wednesday. Hadn't it been at the gas station earlier? Her heart hammered too loud for her to notice much, but yes, she remembered it parked at the gas pump behind her car.

Why was she seeing it everywhere?

Kinda like she'd been running into Jesse. What would he have been doing outside her work? Then at the restaurant on the same night? When she'd been buying ice cream at the grocery store, he'd been there. Had that pickup been in the lot, too?

She sucked in a breath. Jesse had been at the gas station today.

She forced her panic down. She didn't know anything for sure. It was a small town.

A closer look maybe. Leaving the house wasn't an option because she wasn't stupid. All the lights were off, her movements would be hidden. She went into her dad's old bedroom and peered out the window, wondering if she had any binoculars in the house.

A shadow in the driver's seat moved.

She gasped and ducked down.

A dude was in the truck. Was it Jesse? Regardless, some guy sat in his truck down the street.

Dillon popped into her mind. He'd know what to do, but she'd cut him out of her life.

Calling the police would amount to nothing. They might do a drive-by, but it's not like he was breaking the law being creepy. The person in the truck wasn't going to willingly admit to stalking her.

If he was a stalker and if he was stalking *her*. She wasn't the only one who lived on this street. Weirder things had happened, but it was an odd coincidence.

Lifting the curtain, she chanced another peek. Definitely a dude in the truck. Still parked there, which meant he wasn't checking Facebook before he took off after visiting a friend or pulled to the side of a residential street to shoot off a quick text.

There was no else she could call. Besides her father, all of her relationships bordered on acquaintances. There was no way she was dragging Betsy into this. If it was nothing, she'd be a pain in the ass. If it was something, Betsy had children who Elle wouldn't risk exposing to any drama.

Dillon.

Before she could think of all the reasons why not, she'd already dialed his number.

She drew in a shaky breath. What if he was with his new girl?

"Hello?"

Too late. Elle stuttered, words and how to arrange them lost to her.

"Elle? Please tell me you called on purpose and didn't butt dial me and get my hopes up."

Her rising panic won over her vocal cords. "This pickup is sitting outside of my house. I see it everywhere and I'm worried someone's been following me."

"I'll be right over." She heard muffled movements. "Hang up and be prepared to call the police if you need to."

"Okay."

He disconnected.

She kept her phone on the dial pad, occasionally peeking out to see if the truck was still there.

The pickup's lights flashed on. She jumped and dropped her phone. The vehicle pulled away seconds before Dillon's pickup rolled in front of her house.

She ran to the front door and ripped it open just as Dillon trotted up.

"Did you see it?"

He stepped inside, then shut and locked the door. "I did, but I don't recognize it."

"I thought I was overreacting, but he left when you drove up." She shivered. Dillon pulled her close. So familiar, and so good to be held by him again. "How did you get here so fast?"

"I was at the diner on Main. Cash had just left. I was paying to head home."

She pulled back, searching his expression. "You and Cash?"

A faint smile lit his face. "I'd love to tell you all about it, if you'd let me."

She swallowed. Dillon was back in her house. He could do anything, she doubted she'd resist. Except... "Am I taking you away from someone?"

His smile was replaced with a frown. "Just Mama, but I'm past the days of having a curfew. She's probably still out with her friends."

"Oh. I thought— At the gas station, I heard you on the phone, mentioning a girl you wanted to introduce to your mother."

A slow grin spread across his face. "Right. A few new girls. One has soft blonde hair with soulful brown eyes. The other two are kinda wild, but that's good." He winked. "The wild ones catch more mice."

She sputtered. "Cats?"

"No, ma'am. The blonde is Dottie and her bark is literally worse than her bite. She's happy twenty-four/seven like most labs. The other two are cats I rescued, but I like to think they're saving me more than I helped them."

Relief poured through her until giddiness pushed out a chuckle. She laughed and laid her head back down on his shoulder.

He dropped a kiss into her hair. "I'm still holding out

hope for you," he whispered.

Tilting her face to peek up at him, she was unsure of what to say, other than *me, too*. She wouldn't have had the chance anyway. He captured her mouth in a hot kiss.

Her first thought beyond "at last" was that he tasted like sweet tea.

"God, Elle. I dream of you every night and wake up so hard my water bill has tripled from my long showers."

She could relate. She'd had her own moments in the tub, and the desire she fought off then came roaring back. "My bedroom. Now."

He picked her up and carried her toward her room. Laying her down on the bed, he stretched out on top of her.

Yanking his shirt up, she had to work around his hands lifting hers up to her neck. He ripped her bra down, cool air tickled her breasts. His teeth snagged one nipple while he massaged the other breast. Her hands devoured his broad back and shoulders, elated at being able to touch him again.

His erection pressed into her, she arched her hips up into him. She wanted him inside her, cursed herself for using precious time to go to the bedroom. Up against her front door would've been just fine.

Leaving her breast, he kissed up her neck. Their mouths crashed together, tongues demanding hard strokes between licks and nibbles. He pushed his hands under her pajama pants. Rolling her hips up, she encouraged his progress with whimpers to hurry up.

Abruptly, he raised his head and stilled. She was left panting and wanting, his hand resting on her pelvis.

"Did you hear that?" he hissed.

Mystified, she listened. "Someone's driving by?"

"No." He got up, grabbed his shirt and tossed hers to her. "An engine's idling close by. I need to make sure it's not the same guy. Do you have your phone?"

She reached for the nightstand. It wasn't there. "I dropped it in the guest room when you got here."

He pulled his out of his pocket and tossed it to her. She sat up and straightened her clothing as he rushed out of the room.

"Dillon," she whisper-yelled.

"Hey!" His shout came from her front door.

She raced to the door while dialing 9-1-1. The pickup had parked at the end of her driveway running but with all its lights off. Dillon tore across the lawn after a large figure darting back to the truck.

"9-1-1, what's your emergency?"

Elle stifled a yelp in fright when Dillon tackled the man. She spilled every detail possible and rattled off her address.

Knuckles cracked among the growling and wrestling men. She stepped outside, but not any farther. She sniffed. What was that smell?

Gasoline. Dillon's pickup sat in her driveway with a red gas jug tipped over behind it.

Bodies rolled across the driveway. The men grunted, fists hitting flesh smacked through the quiet night. None of her neighbors had noticed, all the houses remained dark. Someone should wake up, help Dillon, but none of them had the experience Dillon had. They'd only get hurt; the same rationale kept Elle planted to her front steps. With a final heave, Dillon pinned the intruder underneath him.

"Elle, did you call the police?" Dillon sat astride the kicking, snarling man, but the guy couldn't break Dillon's hold.

Sirens echoed. Oh thank God.

Two patrol cars turned the corner, flying down the road. They screeched to a halt and the officers jumped out, hands hovering over their weapons.

"This guy was pouring gas all over my truck. He's been stalking Elle." Dillon remained coiled, like he was restraining himself from mashing the intruder's face to a bloody pulp.

"Get up, Dillon," ordered an officer. Elle recognized him from when she'd picked Dillon up from the jail. "Back away with your hands raised. We'll take it from here."

The second officer drew his gun and trained it on the stranger, while the first officer inched forward, instructing him to get up with his hands behind his head.

The man dragged himself to his feet, his nose dripping blood, one eye already swelling shut.

"Jesse," Elle breathed.

"Do you know this guy, Elle?" Dillon asked.

"We kept running into each other. I thought it was coincidence, but it wasn't an accident, was it?" She wanted to look Jesse in the eyes, but his glare remained steady on Dillon.

Jesse spat a mouthful of blood onto her lawn. "I wanted to take everything that fucker had."

"Me?" Dillon's shook his head in disbelief. "What did I ever do to you? We've never met."

"All that land you sit on should be mine. The fancy shit you drive, the nice house you live in, it all should've been mine."

Dillon snorted with derision. "That land's been in my family for generations."

"Not always." Jesse spat again, a bloody glob landing at Dillon's feet. The officer jerked him away to load him in the back of the patrol car.

They drove away, but the second officer, who appeared to be around Dillon's age, stayed behind.

"Hey, Dillon. I need to talk to you and Miss Brady. It might be better if you both come in to the station with me." He jutted his chin toward Dillon's gasoline-drenched pickup. "You can't drive that until it gets washed. Let me call the fire department to see if they can help out."

"Thanks, Scotty." When the officer rolled his eyes at Dillon, he corrected, "Scott. Officer—"

"Anything but Scotty, dude. We aren't in high school anymore."

Elle wrapped her arms around her stomach, her adrenaline crash leaving her sick to her stomach. Dillon strode toward her, a hitch in his step.

"Are you hurt?" She met him halfway, probing his torso like she knew what she was doing. She didn't.

He winced. "I feel fine, but tomorrow I may answer differently." He gave her a lopsided grin, raised a hand to stroke her cheek. "I love you, Elle."

Scott discreetly worked his way to the other side of Dillon's pickup as he took pictures and wrote notes. Elle appreciated the modicum of privacy. If she had been speechless when he answered the phone before, those three words wiped her mind of anything coherent to say. She went from a hopeless, depressed mope to having the man of her too frequent naughty dreams declaring his love on a cool May night in her front yard after a fight.

But then the breakup had been her decision. A decision she'd stood by at the time, but now…

He was the first one she'd wanted to call for help. And he'd come immediately, just like her first instinct had told her he would.

Dillon cleared his throat, looking away. "There's no pressure. Honestly. If you want to take it slow, that's what we'll do. If you want to end things," his throat worked, "I—I'll understand."

Over his shoulder, Scott had finished up with his notes and waited awkwardly for them to finish their discussion.

She grabbed onto that and took the coward's way out. "Let's concentrate on cleaning this mess up before we…" *deal with our mess.* Just because he'd been civil with Cash didn't mean he'd actually changed. If he hadn't, and she gave them another chance, it'd end the same way, and she didn't know if she could recover again.

He gazed deep into her eyes as if judging how she felt about him. He kissed her forehead and murmured, "Whatever you need." He called over his shoulder. "Scott, can I call my cousins in? I think this might involve them."

"Have them meet us at the station. Oh, and the firemen are willing to hose your truck off if, I quote, 'there's a Walker quarter of beef in it for us.'"

Dillon grinned. "Cash will bring some down next week after we butcher."

From a fight on her lawn to bartering beef, it all was beyond her realm of experience. Like her relationship with Dillon.

SCOTT SAT AT HIS DESK, watching Dillon expectantly. It was well after midnight by now and Dillon would rather be in bed. But what Scotty had said temporarily distracted him from the relief that the vandalism was over, there was no more danger toward Elle, and...Elle.

One more minute alone together and he'd have been inside of her. An experience he feared he'd never have again.

When she had been in danger, she'd called him, even thinking he had a new flame.

There was still hope, and he'd hang onto it like a capsized boater hung onto a life raft. The what-ifs plagued him. What if he hadn't been in town? What if that man had tried to get into her house? What if Dillon hadn't been in recovery and had passed out on his couch, completely useless?

"Dillon?" Scott broke in.

One thought of Elle and Dillon's attention had veered off.

His mind spun, recalling what they'd been discussing. "I don't know Scotty—sorry, Scott. The land has always been ours. My Grandpa Walker never mentioned otherwise. I know where I live is one of the newly developed sections, but I assume it was purchased with the rest. I'll have to see what Gram says."

"She never mentioned being married before she met your grandpa?"

Dillon shook his head. They'd always referred to the land as one giant chunk that'd always been in the family, farmed from the very beginning. Their family history had deep roots in Moore.

"I'll visit Gram later today. How many Rodriguezes live in Moore?"

"One family, no relation, but he claimed his grandma's maiden name was McKenzie. That's a common surname around here. Jesse said his great uncle and your grandma married, but he'd passed away within the year, leaving everything to your grandma. Agnes never signed the land back over, despite their requests. They were married, he died, it was hers."

"And Jesse said his grandma and her parents had to leave the county over the feud?"

Scott nodded and steepled his fingers over his desk. "His mom married a Rodriguez. Claims he's the only remaining heir." He spread his hands. "No matter how destitute his family became after moving away from Moore, the land was Agnes's, and now it's yours."

"Legally, he doesn't have a hold on it?" Dillon and his cousins would fight tooth and nail for his property.

"You'd have to consult a lawyer, but my guess is not at all." Scott's gaze landed over Dillon's shoulder. "The rest of your crew is here."

Dillon turned to greet them. "We need to go visit Gram."

CHAPTER 24

*E*lle sat in the rocker at her dad's place, lost in thought. She hadn't talked with Dillon since they separated at the station to give their reports. All his cousins had arrived, so when an officer offered a ride home, she gave in to her exhaustion and accepted.

He'd tried calling on Saturday, but she'd been sleeping. Dillon had to be running on fumes. She doubted he'd stopped to get any rest, judging from the times of his calls. So on Sunday, instead of returning his calls, she'd cleaned up and driven to her dad's. Turmoil tugged at her heart and she'd just needed a friendly shoulder. Since she had few friends, that left her father.

"You gonna tell an old man what's wrong?"

"It's nothing, Dad," she said absently.

He blew a long-suffering sigh. "Peanut, you haven't been the same for weeks. I might not be the most stable individual, but I'm still your father."

She wanted to talk to someone, but her dad was always the one she'd needed to talk to someone about. Confiding in him, even as a teenager, had never been an option. His life had been a mess, consequently affecting hers.

As an adult, she'd been intent on earning a degree to build a better life. When her dad had gotten sick, it hadn't mattered how long he'd been on the wagon, she'd still had to take care of him.

He perched on the chair across from her, not as frail as he'd been months earlier. The consistent care and daily social activities in a controlled environment had done him good. Robust wouldn't describe him, but he looked good. Healthy.

His clear green eyes grew concerned. How long had it been since she'd viewed him as her father and not as a burden?

Before she knew it, the whole story poured out. She held nothing back, stating her exact reasons why Dillon shouldn't be in her future. Her dad remained silent, the pain in eyes obvious, but with no blame. Just regret.

Tears rolled freely as she sobbed. Because she really, really wanted a future with Dillon. And she wanted her dad, *needed* him, because while she spilled her story, she remembered the boxes in her garage, especially the ones he'd stored all his pictures and those newspaper clippings in. He'd been there for her, too. In his broken way, as much as he was able to at the time, he'd always been there.

Swimming tournaments, he'd showed for every one. Bleary eyed and hung over, but he'd never missed them. Graduation. The only pictures she had were the ones he'd taken. College graduation, there'd been no prouder father in attendance. She'd uprooted him from their home, dragged him to Moore "for his own good," and he'd never complained.

Whenever he'd tried to remain sober, it'd been for her. Not for himself, and that was why he'd failed until he'd gotten sick and staying sober had been his decision to live. Until then, he'd done everything for her.

"I'm a horrible person," she cried.

He pulled a chair next to hers. She collapsed into him, he rubbed her back. "No one could've made me prouder than you."

She sobbed harder.

"Your mother met someone new and left us. I blamed myself for so long. For driving your mother away from you."

Wiping her eyes, she remained in his embrace, but calmed herself. He spoke so softly, she could barely hear him.

"When I got sick and finally quit drinking, my thinking cleared. A woman who could walk completely away from her child is more mentally disturbed than I could ever be. I failed you over and over again. I can never make up for it, but I don't have to go back to that behavior." He squeezed harder. "I thanked the doctor last week after the check-up on my hip. Told him I was grateful he discontinued the pain meds."

She sat up, surprised. She'd thought the leukemia was the only reason he quit drinking, that it had given him no choice if he wanted to survive. But he still had a choice and was actively seeking recovery every day.

He handed her a tissue. "As for Dillon...I don't know what to tell you. He seemed like a nice kid, works hard for a living. You glowed around him. But...you gotta do what's best for you."

"I kept pushing him away." Blowing her nose, she attempted to hold the tears back.

"Because you of all people know how it can escalate from there. But Dillon's not me. He has a strong support system, surrounded by people who care for him. He sought help for his problem early, even if it wasn't his idea. Will he continue to struggle?" He shrugged his bony shoulders. "Perhaps. Or... he may not."

Elle groaned, burying her face in her hands. "I've been terribly judgmental."

"You've been cautious," he amended. "For good reason."

"I've been miserable." The last few weeks had been the worst of her life.

"You're smart, beautiful, ambitious. It's my job as a father to point that out. Another man may come along who has his life together, takes care of you, and you might find happiness again."

"You're not making me feel better," she muttered.

"Exactly. I think you already know what you want to do, but you're making yourself dismal resisting. You might get hurt giving him another chance," he smiled, "but it might be worth it."

Sitting back with a sigh, she stared at the ceiling. "When did you get so smart, Dad?" Words he'd always said to her. *When did you get so smart, peanut?* Another thing she'd forgotten in her resentment. She was resilient and driven because he never let her think otherwise.

"Wait until I cook you some spaghetti. You'll marvel over my new kitchen skills."

They ate together and she enjoyed her time with her dad for the first time in over a decade.

DILLON and his four cousins walked into Gram's room for their routine Sunday visit.

She glanced up from the blanket she crocheted, a broad smile spreading across her wrinkled face. "Oh my, what a surprise. I'm afraid the nurses are going to get awfully envious of me again. A few of them would kill to be in this room right now."

His lips twisted in spite of the situation. There weren't enough chairs for all of them, so they all remained standing.

His cousins were just as close to Gram as he was. Cash lived in the house her and Gramps had raised all five boys in. Aaron brought her flowers once a month. During the summer when cold and ice weren't a concern, Travis brought her out for their grilling nights. Brock...well. He was Brock. His visits weren't as routine, but he loved her fiercely.

They all loved her, but today it felt like they were confronting her about something seedy in her past. It was Gram. The most devious thing she'd done were the plates of cookies she'd fed them before sending them home for dinner after chores.

"Good news," Dillon spoke first. "We found the guy who destroyed the shop and my pickup."

"Why, that's good."

Travis cleared his throat. "The thing is Gram," he squatted down in front of her so they weren't all leering over her, "when the police asked him why he did it, he said it was because the land should've been his." Gram's expression turned questioning. "He said his great-uncle married you, and when he passed away, you kept the land Dillon lives on."

Blood drained from her face. Ashen, shaken, she clutched the afghan draped over her legs. "It's preposterous he'd think the land was his."

Aaron finished the rest. "He claimed he's the only one left on that side of the family. He'd grown up hearing about how much better things would've been if his family had stayed here, gotten back what was their son's."

Gram fiddled with the blanket, her mouth working. Anger, disbelief, and regret passed through her wrinkled features. "Harold was a good man."

Dillon exchanged looks with his cousins. None of them had really *believed* Jesse's claims.

"His family was a different story. They were disappointed in me from the beginning. I was a poor girl from town while they owned a beautiful chunk of the county. They had higher hopes for their son. By that, I mean a girl who came with her own land to combine with theirs. They hoped he'd carry them through the rest of their life doing all the work. It's why they had gifted him the land when he'd turned eighteen, otherwise we'd been planning to move, search for our own piece of heaven." Bitterness laced her words. "After Harold and I married, I put my foot down. No way was his family moving in with us so I could raise his sister and be their maid."

She fell quiet.

"What did he die of?" Cash prompted.

Gram fell quiet and stared out the window, her fingers petting the soft fabric of the afghan over her lap. She must've loved Harold, really and truly. "Aneurysm was our best guess. Autopsies weren't as accurate in those days. I was blamed, of course. They fought to kick me off the property, but it was mine." Lifting her hands in a helpless gesture, she appeared ashamed. "The right thing to do would have been to give them the land back. But…it was me being homeless or them, and I justified it at the time, that I wasn't responsible for their house payments. I was going to honor Harold and the farm."

She cackled, her expression mirthful. "It was hopeless. The chickens were eaten by coyotes, the draft horses never listened to me, my milk cow dried up. Harold's family managed to hang onto their house for months, waiting for my imminent failure. Of course the news had spread through town. Your grandfather came to check on me. Helped me." A hint of a smile glossed her face. "He was interested in more than giving me farming lessons from the beginning, but it took me longer to come around." Gazing fondly at the wedding photo of her and their grandpa, she finished the story. "After we married, Harold's family moved and that was the end of it. My property was absorbed by your grandfather. We demolished that old rundown house I inherited from Harold when we knew our kids were going to stay in the business. It...it wasn't an easy decision for me. A lot of memories were in that old place."

Heavy silence settled around the room.

Brock spoke first. "That idiot thought a grudge from sixty years ago gave him the right to drive us out of business?" He shook his head with disgust. "Stupid."

"Explains why I was the only one targeted. He thought I was living his legacy."

Gram's glassy eyes fixed onto the floor. "I always wondered if Harold would've condoned my actions or if he would've thought I acted shamefully."

Travis rubbed her shoulder. "I doubt a man would want his widow to be kicked out of her home, either. You did what you had to do, Gram. It was a bad situation."

Patting his hand, she smiled gratefully. "I...I don't like how Harold's family fared, but my five boys and ten grand-kids make the regret palatable."

"It's been a long day, Gram," Aaron announced. "How 'bout we take you out for dinner?"

None of them wanted to leave her raw, bathing in memories.

She wiped her eyes. "That would be nice."

While Brock and Aaron helped her get ready, Dillon checked his phone. Still nothing from Elle. Each hour that passed lessened his hopes.

He left her one last message. The ball was in her court. Unfortunately, he was afraid she'd let it lay untouched.

CHAPTER 25

*E*lle checked her phone—for the twentieth time that day. It was only three thirty in the afternoon.

Should she call Dillon? He was probably busy with legal issues, catching up on work.

Busy. That's why he hadn't called since he'd left a message. Not because he'd told her he loved her and she'd said nothing in return, hadn't returned his calls. Gah, she wouldn't talk to herself, either.

He was piecing his life back together, staying sober, taking care of his family and the farm. What if he decided he couldn't put up with her lack of commitment and moved on? What if she missed out on them as a couple because she'd let her childhood view of her past dictate her future?

As she ushered her next client in, she wiped out all reflection of her personal life. She had one more session after this and her client deserved her full attention. Still, it wasn't easy. Every fiber of her being vibrated in an effort to run out of her office and make things right with Dillon.

When work wrapped up, she managed an easy walk to her car. She'd meant to drive home, think things through like her normal, logical self. Then, *maybe*, she'd call Dillon and explain her non-reaction to his confession. However, her subconscious won, and instead of calling, she aimed her car toward Dillon's.

It was foolish. He was probably doing farmer duties, out in the field or something. If he was gone, would she just hang out in his driveway?

She totally would. Because on the long drive out to his place, she finally admitted she loved him, too.

Barking greeted her when she pulled up. A young yellow lab, tongue hanging out, tail going wild, danced around her car. Elle guessed Dottie was barely past her puppy days.

Furry shadows disappeared around the house. Those must be the cats Dillon had mentioned.

She parked in the driveway, but remained in the car. Her stomach fluttered with nerves and the part of her that had distanced herself from Dillon since she'd met him urged her to back out and head straight for home.

The front door of the house opened and an attractive woman in her late fifties walked out.

Oh *shit*. Mama. Elle's nerves exploded. Meeting parents was something she'd always avoided with her few past boyfriends. They tended to ask about her personal life. The more she involved herself in a relationship, the harder it was to constantly evade answering.

Elle inhaled a fortifying breath. She was an adult professional and she *could do this*. Even if Dillon rejected her pleas for forgiveness for having no faith in him, or them, his mother was likely a reasonable adult. It was just one woman greeting another. Elle stepped out of the car.

"Hi." She left the door open as an escape route. "Is Dillon around?"

Mama—what was her name?—cocked her head and studied Elle with a pleasant expression. "He ran to town for

— He'll be home in an hour." She covered the distance between them to where Elle stood with a death grip on her open car door. "I'm Christy. Dillon's mama." She said the last word with a rueful smile.

"Elle." She tensed, awaiting judgment.

A knowing expression lit Christy's features. "Nice to meet you, Elle. Listen, I was just taking off to back to Sioux Falls. I threw a roast in for Dillon when he gets home. Why don't you wait inside?"

"Oh, I should've called first." The anticlimactic moment did nothing to douse her nerves.

Christy touched her elbow. "Dillon would rather have you here than miss your call."

The woman's soft touch and reassuring words were everything Elle had missed growing up.

"Are you sure it's okay?" Elle didn't want to face driving back to her house with all of her questions unanswered.

"It's perfect because you can distract Dottie when I leave. We're trying to train her not to run after cars, but she'll ignore it all as soon as I drive off."

The minor duty justified Elle's reason for staying. "What do you need me to do?"

"I'm already packed. I'll pull out of the garage and you can pull in. We'll coax Dottie into the garage and you can stay with her while I shut the door. If that fails, I have dog treats."

Fooling the dog wasn't easy. She was a lab, she loved *everyone*, but she knew Christy and wanted to go with her. Elle wrestled the lunging dog into a bear hug and Christy hit the controls to shut the overhead door.

Elle held Dottie's collar in the garage as the door rolled down. She cooed and rewarded the enthusiastic dog with a treat. By the time Christy's car disappeared, Elle was sweaty and smelled like dog. After several minutes, she opened the garage door to let Dottie run out.

Wishing to tidy up before Dillon arrived, she tested the door to the house that was in the garage. Unlocked. She hesitated. Dottie had run back out into the yard. Were the cats supposed to stay out of the garage?

Just in case, she closed the overhead door before she went inside. She dropped her purse on the table, intending to head to the bathroom, but the fridge caught her eye. Was it really no longer filled with beer?

She resolutely shook her head. Her goal here wasn't to inspect his living conditions. He said he was in recovery, and she either believed him, or she didn't. Elle was lying to herself if she didn't admit to the residual fear of seeing beer lining the shelves. With a sigh, she turned away from the fridge.

The delicious smell of the roast cooking teased her empty stomach. Hoping she'd be invited to stay for dinner, she went to clean up.

DILLON EXITED the church into the cool evening air. He threw a goodbye wave to his sponsor. "See ya next week."

The mental brightness he felt after each AA meeting made it the best hour Dillon spent each week. His first meeting in Moore had gone well. His fear of anonymity had gone out the window. He didn't care if people saw him leave the church every Monday evening and figured out he was in the program. He'd rather be a reflection of the program then a closet drunk.

He glanced at his phone to see a text from Mama. Dammit. She had left a roast in the oven. Plans of finding Elle were curtailed so he could go home to rescue dinner before it dried down to jerky.

It was for the best. Patience was key, and he was willing

to wait as long as Elle needed. He had threatened her career pushing for a relationship and then stomped on her trust when he'd refused to acknowledge his drinking.

Living amends. He could only move forward, doing his best.

Pulling into his yard, he decided to park outside. There were a couple hours of sunlight left. He'd eat and drive out to check the fields, finalize planting plans.

Dottie greeted him when he got out of his truck. Ensuring she didn't lack for attention, he scratched and played with her a few minutes before he figured it was time to take the roast out. He went through his sliding door next to the kitchen and gathered a couple of hot pads. The purse resting on the table didn't register until he set the hot pan on the counter.

Had Mama forgotten her purse? He'd have to call her.

Mid-dial, he heard movement and glanced up, tensed and ready to pounce. Some learned instincts wouldn't die, but he accepted they were a part of his life.

The vision entering the room stole his breath. "Am I imagining things? Did Elle Brady break into my house?"

Her smile was hesitant. "Your mom let me in. Was that okay?"

He soaked in the sight of her, but a part of him warned to keep his happiness in check. "Why are you here?" he asked softly.

Her lovely smiled died and she side-stepped like she was ready to dart around him and run. Wait—was her car in his garage?

He liked the thought too much.

"It's okay." Poor girl looked ready to cry. He wanted to wrap her up in his embrace, but forced himself to stay put. "I don't want to get my hopes up if you're just here to talk about the weekend's excitement."

"I-I just wanted to say…" She swallowed. "That I love you, too, and it terrifies me."

Had he heard right? Again, he wanted to whoop it up, pump his fist, but her confession didn't sound like a good thing to her. He shoved his hands into his pockets so he wouldn't reach for her. "So now what?"

Her gaze darted from him to the roast and back. "Now, I want you to tell me it's going to be okay."

He let his grin spread across his face and crossed to her. She stepped into his embrace before he could pull her in. Her fists twisted into his shirt and she buried her face in his shoulder.

All was right in his world. "It's going to be okay, Elle."

A quick sob escaped and she pulled back. "I'm so sorry—"

He cut her off with a kiss. "Don't. You have nothing to be sorry for. We can talk about what happened, but I understand."

She cupped both sides of his face and brought his head down for a lingering kiss.

He broke apart before they recapped the snowstorm on the floor. "The gentleman in me wants to invite you to sit for dinner, but the man declares the roast will be just as good cold."

"I'll stay for cold roast so you can tell me what happened over the weekend."

He caressed the side of her face. "I want you to stay a lot longer than that."

"I work in the morning, but I can run home for fresh clothes before I go in."

He bent down to swoop her up in his arms. "Good thing farmers are up early, then."

~

ELLE UNLOADED one of the last boxes and pushed it against the wall. There wasn't much that she'd moved to Dillon's house—her house. She blew a tendril of hair out of her eyes. Most of her stuff had been slowly migrating over, but now she was officially moved in. As if she hasn't been staying overnight all summer.

Move in before harvest, otherwise I'll be too busy and in the combine all day until well after dark. And you don't want to haul your stuff in the snow. We'll move you in July because by September, I'll be the phantom sliding into your bed at night.

She smiled at the memory. He swore harvest season meant long days and late nights. And she'd acquiesced to moving in because it was the sensible thing to do. They were together all the time anyway and besides, she'd wanted to.

Much of her worn furniture and used and abused dishes had been donated. Dillon had also cleaned out his drawers and closets to make room for her stuff.

Dillon entered the house behind her.

She spoke without turning around. "I think I'll unpack these tomorrow and make my Sunday exciting. As long as I have my clothes hung up, that's all I really need."

"We should do this one today."

She twisted to check out the box he held.

Chewing her lip, she glanced up at him. The box was the same one she'd found when she was moving her dad. Old family photos, swim awards and medals, and other mementos she'd stuffed away, thinking it was for her own good.

"What are we going to do with them?" What did she want to do with them?

He gave her an encouraging look. "We're going to find places to hang these up. Maybe even put up one with your mom." Her reaction must've been obvious. "Or not. Or it'll hang down in the basement. Whatever you're comfortable with. But *your* stuff is going to hang on these walls and decorate any shelves I can find."

Grudgingly, she smiled. "You're incredibly thoughtful—and demanding."

She sauntered over to him. They'd been moving all day and cleaning her house so she could give up the rental. Watching Dillon in action, with his strong body…

He stepped back. "Oh no. You're not distracting me with seduction."

"I'm doing no such thing!"

"You are, but I'm not letting you touch me until this box is empty."

He knew her too well. That box by itself was no big deal. Displaying the items in that box pushed her out of her comfort zone.

"Fine," she grumbled.

For the next hour, he diligently pounded nails and hung frames. The more she walked past her pictures hanging on the walls, the more comfortable and accepting she was. Dillon peppered her with questions about each item.

Before long, she was telling him stories from growing up and from her swim days. Sure, there were many bad moments during those years, and she remembered them all clearly, but dusting off the happy memories wasn't as painful as she'd expected.

She scooted closer to him and whispered. "Can I touch you now?"

The box was empty. Her old house was empty, but Dillon's place, *their* place, was full of love and promise.

BROCK'S A MAN who's better with an engine than he is with a woman. Until he runs down a sexy trespasser and tackles the only girl who takes the time to understand him in Mustang Summer.

THANK YOU FOR READING. I'd love to know what you thought. Please consider leaving a review of Conflict of Interest at the retailer the book was purchased from.

FOR ALL THE LATEST NEWS, sneak peeks, quarterly short stories, and free material sign up for my newsletter.

ABOUT THE AUTHOR

Marie Johnston writes paranormal and contemporary romance and has collected several awards in both genres. Before she was a writer, she was a microbiologist. Depending on the situation, she can be oddly unconcerned about germs or weirdly phobic. She's also a licensed medical technician and has worked as a public health microbiologist and as a lab tech in hospital and clinic labs. Marie's been a volunteer EMT, a college instructor, a security guard, a phlebotomist, a hotel clerk, and a coffee pourer in a bingo hall. All fodder for a writer!! She has four kids, an old cat, and a puppy that's bigger than half her kids.

mariejohnstonwriter.com
Facebook
Twitter @mjohnstonwriter